I0788407

LULU AND BETTY:
GROWING UP IN CHANGING TIMES

By

Patricia Sawyers Fiske

LULU AND BETTY:
Growing Up In Changing Times

By
Patricia Sawyers Fiske

Published By
Positive Imaging, LLC
9016 Palace Parkway
Austin, TX 78748
bill@positive-imaging.com

All Rights Reserved

Contents

DEDICATION

To my granddaughter, Maria Russinovich. She embodies the spirit of the millions of young people of her generation, who are championing great causes, demanding answers, and marching for action from our government. They give me hope for the future of America.

FOREWORD

Our story about Betty and Lulu, who grew up in peaceful times, begins in 1933, during the depression, and ends in the early forties as prosperity returned, as our country began mobilizing for World War II.

I started this book because I thought it would be beneficial for young people, like my talented granddaughter, Maria, to contrast growing up during the past seventy-five years, with my formative years, a time of peace, from 1927-1941.

Our childhoods were so very different. I've watched my granddaughter entertain herself with technology from an early age. While she missed knowing about doodlebugs, she can always look them up on her I-Phone or laptop. From a very early age, she was aware of world events; whereas, I didn't realize that my back yard in Kerrville, Texas, was not the center of the Universe until I started to school.

1

GETTING ACQUAINTED

Summer, 1933 - Kerrville, Texas

"Doodlebug, doodlebug, your house is on fire." eight-year-old Betty chanted as she stirred the loose soil with a stick.

"Whatcha doin'?" came a nearby voice.

Betty was startled to see a little girl she didn't know standing nearby.

"Who are you?" Betty blurted.

"I'm Louise Sawyers, but everyone calls me Lulu. Betty stood up to get a better look at the intruder and realized that she was taller than Lulu. "How old are you?

"I'm six, going on seven." Lulu answered.

"Well I'm Betty Brown and I'm eight, going on nine."

"So, whatcha doin'? Lulu repeated.

"I'm getting a doodlebug to come out of it's house."

"How'd you know where to find it's house?" asked a puzzled Lulu.

"That's easy. That bug is so dumb, it leaves a hole that's shaped like an ice cream cone, on the roof and points to where it lives. See, there's one."

Both girls were on their knees by now, their bare toes digging into the soft sand, staring at the inverted cone in the soil. Betty handed Lulu a small stick. "Now stir up that hole and say what I say. Doodlebug, doodlebug your house is on fire."

Lulu did as she was told and soon bits of sand came shooting from the hole. Lulu held her breath and Betty laughed as a tiny creature emerged from the hole backwards. It had a tiny head and forearms, but a large abdomen and hind legs. It was the color of the soil, so it was difficult to see. Lulu gasped and Betty whispered, "Now watch what happens."

The tiny insect began repairing the damage done to its house. Soon it burrowed back into the point of the cone and all was just as it was before Lulu had disturbed it. She grabbed the stick to repeat the process, but Betty said, "It'll just do the same thing. I'm tired of this. Let's play cars. My mom works for this rich lady that has grandkids that are grown and she gives my mom their old toys and yesterday, she brought home these two metal cars."

Before Lulu could answer, a slightly older girl appeared at the back door of Betty's house calling, "Betty, where are you? It's your turn to get the eggs."

"Is not. I gottum last time," yelled Betty as she jumped up and stood with her hands on her hips.

Julia, Betty's 16-year-old sister, Had the same sandy hair as Betty, but hers was neatly combed with two braids and Betty's was a mass of unruly curls. Julia started down the stairs calling, "I fed the chickens this morning, so it's your turn to get the eggs."

Betty turned to Lulu, "aw shucks, I wanted to play cars."

"Me too. Who's she?" asked Lulu.

"That's just my crabby sister, Julia."

"You better hurry, 'cause Mom'll be home soon, and you better be more careful. You broke two eggs last time," Julia shouted, as she went back up the stairs and slammed the back door.

Betty dropped the cars and turned toward the chicken yard in back of the house. Looking back over her shoulder, she asked Lulu, "Ya wanna help?"

"Sure," Lulu enthused as she followed Betty through the back gate that led to the henhouse, but when they got there and Betty grabbed a bucket and went in, Lulu stayed outside, looking in. She didn't like the smell of chicken poop, or the noises coming from inside the chicken house. She watched as Betty deftly reached under each hen for the day's egg crop and laughed when the hens squawked and pecked at Betty. Betty finished gathering the eggs and stepped out of the henhouse.

Lulu gasped, "Oooh, you have doodoo all over your feet."

Betty started back to the house. "It'll wash off. I'm used to it now." When they reached the faucet, Betty scrubbed the soft, smelly feces from her feet with a brush kept there for that purpose.

Lulu hated the smell and was grateful when an inviting new aroma reached her nostrils as they reached the gate, which was covered with fragrant honeysuckle. The stench of the henhouse finally faded.

"You've got a lot of chickens," Lulu observed.

"Yeah, we sell a lot of eggs, and eat them most every meal. Geraldine thinks we should eat the chickens, cuz she hates eggs."

"Who's Geraldine?" quizzed Lulu.

"My second oldest sister. She's fourteen."

"How many sisters do you have?" asked a curious Lulu.

"Four. There's also Bernice. She's ten, and Mary Lou, whose twelve."

"And you all live here in this little house?"

"Yep, and my mom makes six. How many live at your house?"

Lulu thought a bit, "Right now just four. My mom, my granny, my sister, Dorothy, and me.

I have a brother too, Jim. He's seven years older than Dorothy, and Dorothy is seven years older than me. My aunt Vera said my mom had a seven-year-itch. Jim left home when we still lived in the big house on Lytle Hill. "

"We used to live in a big house too, with servants and everything," interrupted Betty.

"When granddaddy was alive, we had servants too, but when he died, we had to move here near you. It gets pretty crowded sometimes when my daddy comes home from working on some bridge for the WPA."

"What's the WPA?" puzzled Betty.

"I don't know, but my mom says that President Roosevelt started it to save us from the depression, whatever that is."

Mention of moms reminded Betty of her job. "Listen, I gotta get these eggs ready to deliver, so I gotta go."

She was about to leave when Lulu called, "Maybe we can play cars tomorrow."

"Sure", said Betty as she closed the screen door.

Lulu's Granny

Lulu ambled slowly to her new home near Betty's house. Her mother had sent her out to play earlier because she was making too much noise and waking her sick granny. But it was almost time for supper and Lulu was hungry, so she tiptoed into their small apartment.

She could tell that her mother was still in a bad mood, so she tried to be invisible, but it didn't work.

"There you are. Where have you been?" Before Lulu could answer, her mom ordered, "Your granny's spit can is full. Go empty it." This is the reason Lulu tried to stay outside as much as possible. She hated having to empty the smelly spit can.

"Mama, that ain't fair. It's Dorothy's turn. I did it last time and granny doesn't even like me." sassed Lulu.

"Isn't fair, Lulu." corrected Lulu's mother, "And your grandmother loves both my girls."

Lulu's Granny, whose maiden name was Lula Mae Harris, was bedridden and, when Lulu's grandfather died, she came to live with Lulu's family in homes where they rented an apartment. Living in other peoples' homes became a pattern for her family most of Lulu's childhood. The depression was still going on and many widows or elderly couples helped make ends meet by renting parts of their homes to others. It allowed people to live in nicer neighborhoods than they could otherwise afford. After Lulu's father went into construction work, they could only afford two bedrooms, so, Lulu, being the youngest, slept on day beds and sofas, mostly in living rooms, until she was out of college.

Lulu's household revolved around her granny's illness. Granny was tall and emaciated. Her pale skin was taut over protruding bones, reminding Lulu of skeletons. She had short dark hair brushed back away from her face emphasizing her cadaverous appearance.

She had her own room and Lulu's mother took care of all her needs, which is why she was always tired and grouchy. Lulu did pretty much as she liked, as long as she was quiet, so as not to bother her granny.

Lulu found her granny's snuff-dipping disgusting. She watched as her granny would pull out her lower lip and dump a brown powder out of this small round tin between her lower gums and lower lip, then mull it around for a while in her toothless mouth. Then she would pull a large, Folgers coffee can from under her bed and spit this slimy, brown substance into the can.

There was also the necessity for what was called, a "slop jar" as it was too far for her to go to the bathroom. This was a bucket that fitted into a hole in a wooden chair. It had a round handle for carrying. Sometimes Lulu was asked to take these containers into the bathroom and empty them into the toilet, but she made so much fuss, her mother didn't often ask. Today she did. Lulu was about to have a tantrum when her sister, Dorothy, appeared.

Lulu whined, "It's your turn to take out the spit can and mama told me to. It's not fair."

"Oh, you're such a baby. I'll do it so I won't have to listen to you carry on." Dorothy volunteered.

Friends Forever

That night, Lulu dreamed of playing cars with her new friend. The next morning, she woke up early, thinking about Betty and the prospect of playing cars. She followed her mother around the small kitchen as she prepared breakfast. Hoping to hurry the process, she babbled stories about her new friend. When her mother finally put her food on the table, she bolted it and started for the door.

"Wait a minute miss priss. Where do you think you're going?" her mother called.

"Over to Betty's. We're gonna play cars." Lulu called over her shoulder. Then she was out the door. Lulu's mother didn't object. Her sick mother was still asleep and she needed some time to herself.

To get to Betty's house, Lulu had to cut through Vernon's yard, which was between Lulu's and Betty's. Vernon's folks had a cow, which they kept in a pen behind their house. There was a short-cut between Vernon's house and the cow pen, which Lulu took as the cow was at the other end of the pen.

Lulu ran the short distance to Betty's deserted yard and decided to knock on the back door. Betty appeared shortly, and smiled. "Hi, what's up?"

"You said we could play cars today." panted Lulu.

"Yeah, but I have to feed the chickens first. It's my turn. Wanna help?"

"Sure, show me how." Lulu said as she started down the steps, following Betty.

They quickly went to the henhouse where Betty got a bucket and filled it with little pellets of chicken feed, which she handed to Lulu. "I'll let the hens out and fill the water trough." instructed Betty. "Just be sure the gate is closed first, and then toss the chicken feed all over the ground outside the henhouse."

Lulu began spreading the feed enthusiastically, spilling a lot at her feet, so when Betty let the hens out, they crowded around Lulu, pecking her toes at times. She had never been around chickens, so Lulu found this very exciting and a little scary and Betty found Lulu's antics hilarious.

Still laughing, Betty turned off the water and started for the gate. "They'll be ok as long as the food lasts. Remind me to put them back in their house later."

"Now can we play cars? an eager Lulu asked.

Betty's mother had appeared on the back porch. "I gotta say goodbye to my mom first. She has to go to work." explained Betty as she ran to the back steps, leaving Lulu to close the gate.

"Now, be a good girl and mind Julia." Her mother instructed.

"She's so bossy, mom," whined Betty.

"I know dear, but she has a lot of responsibility for a sixteen-year-old."

"Why can't Geraldine be in charge?"

"Because she's only 14 and I need her to do the cooking, and Mary Lou to do the shopping. Betty we've been over this too much. You know we all need to do our part to make this family of girls work," Betty's mother patiently explained.

"I know," Betty conceded, "but why do Bernice and me do all the dirty work?"

"Betty dear, taking care of the chickens is the most important job of them all. Without the eggs, we wouldn't have enough to eat or the money to buy what we need. Now give me a kiss, I have to get to work." The young widow Brown, as she was known to her neighbors even though she had a first name - Ellen, made last minute adjustments to her clothes and makeup as she delivered this speech to her youngest daughter.

Lulu stood open-mouthed during this exchange. She couldn't understand why Betty's mother looked so much younger and prettier than her own. The young widow had a quiet beauty. She was slender and average height, sandy-haired, and well-groomed, with a pleasing demeanor. Lulu listened to the patient way that Betty's mother explained things and wished that her own mother was not so grumpy all the time.

As Betty gave her mother a dutiful kiss on the cheek, her mother remembered as she turned to go, "And don't forget, it's your turn to clean up the kitchen."

Betty slumped to the steps saying, "Aw shucks."

Lulu was all sympathy, "You sure have to do a lot around here."

"We all do, since my daddy died," moaned Betty. "The kitchen can wait. Let's play cars!"

Lulu was elated, "At last," she thought.

The two young friends found a shady place, where the former tenants had a garden, to play cars. The dirt would be easy to dig there and it was away from the house and chicken yard.

Ever resourceful, they decided that a car needed a garage, which they created by digging a space in the dirt for the car and improvising a roof with sticks. They then expanded the game. "Pl'ike we live next door to each other. My house will be here and you --" Lulu said.

Betty interrupted, "No, I want my house there, next to my garage."

The bickering continued until they finally agreed and busily set about building magnificent edifices out of dirt, stones, and anything that would lend itself to the project.

This filled most of that week, because they felt the need to build houses for their friends as well. Then, of course, they needed roads, and that demanded a filling station. Their fertile minds created never-ending stories and adventures, which they enacted in their village - weddings, robberies, funerals, etc. Sometimes they used sticks for people, but mostly, they used dolls of all sizes to enact their dramas. Often the doll was larger than the car it was supposed to be riding in.

"I just heard on the radio that some robbers stole a lot of money from Shriner's Bank, and they haven't caught 'em yet." an excited Betty told Lulu. " I'll bet we could catch 'em. I'll be the cops."

"Ok, and I'll be the robbers . Lulu grabs her car and quickly rolls it down one of the roads they had made."

Betty immediately starts making siren noises and follows with her car, "You better stop, or I'll shoot."

"Yeah, well, I'll shoot back."

They start going pow, pow, when Betty yells, "Look out, you're going to hit that train!"

Sure enough, Lulu crashes her car into a toy train that is on a track they had made the day before.

Betty yells, "Don't let 'um getaway!"

"They can't, Lulu says, "they're both dead."

They had many versions of this event, with the bad guys always meeting a bad end. The truth is that the real robbers got away. The police chief said it was because the only police car in Kerrville was so old and slow. Actually, Officer Murphy pursued the thief all the way into the next county, only to lose the culprit, when the patrol car ran out of gas.

By summer's end, they had an entire village, with churches, a police station, schools, and all manner of stores - drug stores, grocery stores, etc. All this activity, crawling around on the ground, left knees with scabs and fingernails permanently filthy.

By this time, Betty and Lulu were fast friends with a daily routine involving, not just cars, but all types of diversions.

Tarzan and Jane

Climbing trees and playing Tarzan was one of their favorite pastimes. Betty had a huge chinaberry tree that overhung her house. The neighborhood children often had competitions as to who could hang upside down the longest. They usually hung with our knees hooked over a large limb, and toes hooked under another nearby limb to secure them.

Lulu had large feet and decided to outdo the others by hanging by one foot. The contest winner got to be Tarzan and Lulu didn't want to be Jane or Cheetah, so she found a place where two limbs met in a 'v' and wedged her foot in the apex. The problem with that was that she had done too good a job in securing her foot, so she couldn't get loose when she was finally declared winner. The blood rushed to her head and she was in trouble. Fortunately, an older boy, named Harris, was playing with them that day and he was able to hold

Lulu's weight while others extricated her foot from its vice. He became her hero, and Lulu conceded that Harris would be Tarzan and she would be Jane.

Betty and Lulu had a club house under a huge fig tree in the Brown's chicken yard. They cleared a space that was hidden from prying eyes by the fig tree's abundant branches. This space served as an outdoor home, where they played dolls, and sometimes, became a school, when they played teacher.

It was their secret place. They had a secret password, 'figgy', and a secret sign, which consisted of putting one fist over the other as though you were climbing a rope.

It was understood that neither girl would disclose their special place to anyone, but Tarzan wanted to be alone with Jane, and she couldn't resist taking Tarzan inside the clubhouse. She wrote the following poem years later about what happened.

You Tarzan—Me Jane

While pondering the source of my passion for trees,
Conjure childhood. "Me Tarzan" cavorting in breeze.
Mid purple chinaberry blossoms, in panties I'd swing
fearlessly defying gravity, swing like bird on the wing.
Not yet in school, little girls keeping cool, climbing high,
playing Tarzan, so innocently, scantily clad. Though I try,
I can't remember the day when Harris joined our game,
but, from the day he spoke that word, it wasn't the same.
First, he usurped me as Tarzan, said I ought to be Jane.
Other girls would be Cheetah or be left out in the rain.
He was older, you see. He should have been in school.
I learned years later, why he could break a golden rule.
Just like in the movies, Tarzan's arms twined round Jane.

He explored round her jungle, as they hid down the lane.
He sang a song from the Hit Parade they both had heard,
"Soon, the two of us will—." He whispered a bad word.
She didn't know its meaning, but she liked his secret tone,
looked forward to what it was that they would do alone.
They sang the song furtively, both whispering the last part.
Cheetah seemed to always be around, so they must resort
to subterfuge to find privacy at some other time and place.
She waited long at a rendezvous, never ever saw his face.
Years went by, her secret was sealed deep inside her soul.
Sharing a four-letter word cast her in scarlet-woman role.
You may laugh at her reaction to a word used round town
as verb, adjective, adverb, expletive, and often even noun.
The thirties had propriety and some words carried stigma,
cheap and crude if uttered, thus explaining Jane's enigma.
She carried guilt for years for words and gropes in jungle.
God would surely punish her for her part in that bungle.
She'd done little wrong, yet she hid her guilty knowledge.
Secrets stayed locked in her heart until she was in college.
She learned from his brother why Tarzan missed their date.
Sent to a sanatorium, he kept a more urgent date—with fate.
Some trivial deeds loom large if hidden until we are gray.
Jane carried that shameful secret, locked inside until today.

Vernon and the boys

Vernon was the ringleader of the neighborhood boys who played games with their homemade rubber-guns. They played 'cops and robbers' and 'cowboys and Indians,' but never 'war'. Our country was at peace and did not have wars being touted on the radio every day.

Vernon's dad helped the boys saw the crude shape of a gun from a flat board, which was sawed from the end of a fruit crate acquired from the local grocer, Mr. Butt. HEB started in Kerrville, Texas.

The handle and long barrel were cut in one piece. On the back of the handle, they attached a clothes pin, the kind you squeezed together to open.

Tires then, looked like today's tires, but they had to have an 'inner-tube' inside to keep them inflated. It looked like the innertubes we float in on the river, but they were made of heavy-duty rubber.

They then found an old tire inner- tube, cut it into sections about a half-inch wide to make ammunition. The tube section was secured on the end of the barrel, then was pulled taught. The other end was put in the vise of the close pin. When the clothes pin trigger was pulled, the rubber 'bullet' sped to it's target, usually one of the girls' behind. Girls were allowed to play with the boys, only if they would be a robber or Indian.

Julia always volunteered to be a squaw, because she had a crush on Vernon, and he always chose her behind as his target, because he felt the same about her.

Indoor Games. 1934

On cold or rainy days they were confined to Betty's living room, because they were not allowed to play in the rest of the house. This was not all bad, because the radio was there on a table. It was made of wood, with a curved dome. On it's face was a small lit area showing a dial and stations that could be heard by turning a knob on the front of the radio. There was another knob that you could turn to regulate the sound.

Betty and Lulu would listen to shows like, Jack Armstrong, the All American Boy, Little Orphan Annie, The Green Hornet, and The Shadow Knows. Sometimes, when Mrs. Brown was at home, they were trapped into hearing a soap opera, like Stella Dallas.

On those days, when not playing with dolls, the girls were cutting out paper dolls from old Sears and Roebuck catalogs. They would find a full model from the lingerie section, paste it on a piece of cardboard, color it, and cut it out.

Then they would find clothes in the clothing section that would fit that paper doll. In cutting out the clothes, they would make tabs on the shoulders that could fold over and thus keep the garment on the model. They even got Vernon's dad to make little stands with a slot in them to hold the paper-doll upright.

By the end of the day, each paper doll had a huge wardrobe for all occasions. The friends would then create the occasions and stories for the paper dolls to act out.

Sometimes, when they couldn't go outside, they played cards and other games. Lulu liked card games, like Old Maid and Go Fish, which required very little thought or talent, and she could sometimes win.

Betty's choice of games were Pick-up-sticks and jacks. These were games requiring skill and coordination, which eight-year-old Betty had, but Lulu's six-year-old muscles hadn't mastered and she always lost.

Neither the widow nor Lulu's mother had supplied them with the facts of life, so they had to rely on what Betty's older sisters told them.

One day, Betty, Geraldine, her older sister, and Lulu, were in their kitchen eating watermelon and gossiping. "Have you seen Jenny's mom lately? Her stomach is way out to here," Betty gestured with her arms bowing out in front of her stomach.

One wonders if Geraldine didn't know about childbirth or if she was teasing them, but she told Betty and Lulu that the woman had swallowed a watermelon seed, and it had grown into a watermelon in her belly, and the only way she could get it out of her stomach would be to push the melon out through the hole where we poop. Betty and Lulu squealed in horror. They both agreed that pooping a watermelon would hurt.

That night Lulu had nightmares about a giant plant growing inside of her, with stems pushing out her ears and eyeballs and a melon that got bigger and bigger until she exploded.

The next day Lulu went to see Betty to tell her about her dream and was told that she was in the bathroom. They had no inhibitions about seeing each other on the toilet, so Lulu went into the bathroom unannounced. Betty was sitting on the toilet, crying.

Before Lulu could ask, "What's the matter?" Betty sobbed that she had swallowed a watermelon seed and was trying to poop it out before it started growing in her. She got Lulu's full sympathy as she strained until her face turned red.

Betty's dilemma was solved a bit later when her oldest sister, Julia, needed to use the bathroom. When Betty told her why she needed to stay on the toilet until she pooped the seed, Julia laughed. "You silly goose, Geraldine is full of prunes. Jenny's mom didn't swallow a watermelon seed. That's a baby in her stomach. She is going to have a baby and you're too young to have a baby. Now, get up. I need to go bad."

Relieved that she wouldn't grow a watermelon in her belly, Betty and Lulu spent the rest of the day speculating on how the woman got a baby into her stomach and how she could ever get it out.

For the next two years, Betty and Lulu played daily after school and in the summer, they were inseparable, but shortly after their second summer as playmates ended, Lulu's granny died and things changed.

Granny's Death, 1935

Lulu's landlady allowed the family to use the living room, which was between her part of the house and ours. Lulu was forbidden to enter it, but her mother was so busy nursing her granny, she never noticed how often Lulu sneaked in. It was her sanctuary. The big fascination was the bookshelf filled with all manner of books. Lulu's family's only book was the family bible. Although she could not yet read the many books, Lulu soaked up the illustrations, making up stories about what she saw. Her fascination with books, begun in that musty room, never dimmed.

It was always dark and dusty in there as it was seldom used by anyone. Lulu enjoyed secret trysts with her book friends for some time until, one day, she thought she saw the bookshelf move, which evoked images of ghosts or worse, thus ending her visits until the day of her granny's death.

That day, the living room, Lulu's former sanctuary, was transformed. The lights were on and people were sitting around the room on the many chairs which Lulu had always seen empty. A large group of sympathetic friends listened to Lulu's mother loudly lamenting granny's departure. Lulu wondered why her mom wasn't a bit relieved after all her years of constant work and caring.

Uncomfortable among all the people gathered to say goodbye to granny in that room so full of scary memories, Lulu sneaked into the bedroom where her Granny lay on a high gurney, covered by a large sheet that showed the contours of her bony body. Lulu wanted to pull the sheet from her face so she could breathe. There was an oscillating fan blowing the sheet making it seem that she was still alive and moving. Lulu let out a shriek and ran back into the room where all were gathered.

She was quickly turned over to her favorite uncle, Hoot, who was supposed to drive her to Martha Nell Beddingfield's birthday party, which happened to be that day.

Lulu's cousin Willa Mae's, husband, Hoot, was her favorite relative and he was always putting her on his lap and tickling her, which made her move a lot. When they got into the car, he put Lulu in his lap and let her pretend to drive. She rewarded him by squirming often due to a hard object in his lap.

Years later when she was in College and wiser, Hoot and his wife visited Lulu's family. His fully erected hug made her realize what that hard object in his lap, when she was little, had been.

Moving On

When two days passed after the funeral without a visit from Lulu, Betty got worried and went over to Lulu's to see what the problem was. She found Lulu huddled on her porch, crying.

"Don't cry Lulu, she's better off in heaven. She won't be sick anymore."

That stopped the tears.

"That's not why I'm crying, silly. Mama says we have to go live with daddy in Austin now that granny doesn't need her anymore."

This news caused Betty to sink down on the steps beside Lulu." Oh, no. we'll never see each other again." Betty moaned.

With that thought, they both began to cry. Soon, Lulu's mother came out to try to calm them down. "Now, don't go getting all upset. We won't be going right away. Lulu needs to finish this school year here before we move."

Lulu's mother sits down on the steps next to Betty. " It's been a long time since I had time to just sit." She pats Betty on the knee, " So this is Betty, I've certainly heard a lot about you. Lulu seems to think you hung the moon."

"Oh, she knows better than that. She's real smart for her age." Betty allowed. Lulu's mother seemed nicer than Betty expected.

Lulu is not sure she likes this conversation, but she sits down next to Betty.

" Betty, maybe you can satisfy my curiosity. I see this man in a big, fancy car pick your mother up in the morning and bring her back by supper time. He looks very familiar." Lulu's mother is not the only neighbor who wonders.

"Yes m'aam, you probably saw Mr. Marshal down at Schreiner's bank. He owns it. My mom works for him, taking care of his sick wife." Betty answers.

She is interrupted by Lulu, who objects to the third degree her mother is conducting. "Let's go play, I'm tired of this talking." She is going down the steps headed for Betty's house before her mother can object.

"I guess I had better go too," Betty said as she stood up.

Lulu's mom nodded in agreement, "It's been nice talking with you."

"Thanks," called Betty as she ran to catch up with Lulu.

"Where you heading, Lulu?"

"I dunno", was Lulu's answer.

"Let's go to our clubhouse. I have something private to tell you," whispered Betty.

Once the two girls settled in their favorite spots, Betty confided, "remember when I thought I'd swallowed a watermelon seed and Julia told us about having babies. We wondered how the baby got in there in the first place. Well, my mom explained it all to me. I can't remember the big words she said, but I get the picture. A baby starts with a seed, too, but it gets in the woman's stomach when a man puts his thing in her pussy and plants the seed in her."

Lulu gasped, "Oh my goodness. If I had let Harris do what he wanted to, I could have had a baby."

"I don't think so. My mom says a girl has to be menis---uh, she has to bleed between her legs every month before she can have a baby, explained Betty.

A puzzled Lulu mumbled, "I don't understand."

"Remember, I told you about how Julia has to plug herself up every month when she bleeds to keep the blood from running down her leg and getting on everything. My mom says that'll happen to me pretty soon, so I need to tell her if I see blood on my panties. She says it happens to all girls," was Betty's attempt to explain.

"Ooooh!" was all Lulu could muster.

"Your mom will probably explain this to you when you get a little older," offered Betty.

Lulu countered, "I doubt it. Let's change the subject. ...I'll really miss this."

"And I'll miss you, "an equally wistful Betty replied. "But we have the rest of the school year together."

"And we'll see each other every Christmas, 'cause we always spend the holidays with my Aunt Vera in her big house here in Kerrville." Lulu offered.

Betty jumped in, "And we can write to each other in between."

Lulu threw cold water on that one, "Yeah, but that won't make up for missing out on our summers together - playing cars, climbing trees...." Her voice trailed off as she fought back the tears.

Betty was about to cry as well, when she remembered that she was now ten and needed to set an example for her younger friend, who was only eight. "Come on Lulu. Cheer up. We have til school's out, so let's have fun while we can. Let's play circus. I'll be the clown." Betty makes silly faces and waddles out of the clubhouse, followed by Lulu imitating her waddle.

34

2

LULU MOVES TO AUSTIN

1936

The school year flew by with both girls trying to enjoy the time left for them to be together. When the day came for Lulu to leave, Betty forgot about setting an example and joined Lulu in tearful vows of friendship forever, and impulsively gave Lulu a tender kiss that awakened feelings in Betty that she had never felt.

That summer was spent by Betty in the same surroundings, doing the same things, but with Lulu gone she felt a sense of sadness. She thought often of the feelings aroused by that last kiss and wondered if Lulu felt that arousal too.

Lulu, however, had little time to reminisce as each day brought new people and situations to occupy her mind. Before moving to Austin, Lulu's father had rented an apartment in a widow's home in Hyde Park. The widow told them of a summer program for children at a nearby park. The day Lulu's mother took her to sign up for the program, she learned that they were casting a play about Snow White the next day. Lulu was thrilled as she loved nothing more than playing make believe.

Lulu was glad to have someplace, beside the crowded apartment, to spend her time and loved showing off, so she tried out for the play and got the part of the wicked queen.

She was thrilled when the audience reacted to her wickedness. She wrote Betty about the experience. "Last night I went to the edge of the stage and scared a little girl on the front row. I looked at her real mean and pointed my finger right in her face when I said, "I'll tell the hunter to find Snow White, and KILL her". The little girl screamed and ran to her Mommy." This experience planted a seed for acting that grew and flourished throughout Lulu's life.

Betty wrote Lulu, "I wish I could have been there when you made that little girl scream. I've got lots of news. Remember Tarzan, they put Harris in the sanatorium, 'cause he has TB." And, I guess I need to stay away from boys, 'cause I started bleeding and I don't want any seeds planted in me. She closed her letter with, "I can't wait til Christmas to kiss you again." Lulu thought that might be some kind of joke.

Christmas at Aunt Vera's

Lulu had mixed emotions about the annual Christmas celebration at her aunt's house. She loved the delicious food that her family could not afford, and she looked forward to seeing her friend, Betty. On the other hand, Lulu hated the role of poor relations that her family fell into. Vera's family exchanged lavish gifts among themselves and gave token gifts to Lulu's family. Lulu's mother usually gave homemade gifts or home cooking to Vera's family. Lulu found this humiliating, but even worse was the belittling attitude of Vera's son, Patrick. He criticized Lulu's table manners, the way she dressed and the way she talked. His sarcastic barbs made Lulu wish they had never come to Kerrville.

Kerrville was a small town and gossip traveled fast. As soon as Lulu and her family arrived, Lulu's aunt couldn't wait to pass the latest on. The gossip was that, somewhere along the line, the widow Brown's high morals had slipped a bit. She didn't own a car, but several nights a week, a big, green Buick pulled up by a vacant lot across the street. Someone happened to be looking, saw the widow take an indirect route to the car and quickly get in. Well, gossip was rampant that the driver was Bruce Marshall, a prominent, businessman, who was married and lived in the rich part of town. One nosey neighbor took it upon himself to follow Mr. Marshall and the widow one night. They went to a small, isolated house on the outskirt of town, stayed several hours before returning to the place where the widow had been picked up. She was seen throwing a kiss as Mr. Marshall drove away. There had been rumors before, but now the widow became a 'scarlet woman' in the eyes of that small-town community. The effects of the gossip even spread to the schools, where the widow's five girls suffered shaming and ostracism.

After Lulu's mother heard the gossip, she refused to let Lulu go to Betty's house, but said that it was alright for Betty to come to the aunt's house. That was arranged, but the visit did not go well. Every time the girls started having fun like they had always done, someone shushed them. Then Lulu's cousin Patrick began making rude remarks like, "What kind of friends would you expect poor relations to have?" They would have gone outside, but it was too cold, and they couldn't find a place where they weren't under scrutiny. They were both relieved when it was time for Betty to go home. For Betty it was an opportunity to get another kiss from Lulu, but Lulu was uncomfortable and pushed her away.

3

SAN ANTONIO

1937

On the ride back to Austin, Lulu's dad told them that he was taking a better job in San Antonio, so Lulu got to complete the school year in Austin and move to San Antonio at the first of the next summer.

Lulu was sorry to miss out on the summer play ground program with the possibility of being in another play, but she wouldn't miss her penmanship class at school. The students were expected to master cursive writing using a dip pen in an ink well despite the fact that no one used those anymore.

They moved to a residential neighborhood in San Antonio, fortunately near a playground where there were supervised programs and activities for neighborhood children. Lulu soon had another chance to be on stage. She managed to get herself involved in an upcoming Valentine Day program singing *Let me Call you Sweetheart* to a young lady. They were to be silhouetted so Lulu could pass as a boy.

She had been rehearsing for weeks and was so excited to be on stage again. Unfortunately, her parents had other plans the night of the performance and refused to let her perform. They didn't tell her until almost show time, so she didn't even have an opportunity to let the director know that she wouldn't be able to perform.

Another Move

The reason Lulu's parents didn't let Lulu perform is that her father was moving on to another job outside of San Antonio and they needed to find a different place for Lulu and her mother to live as her mother would not have a car and they needed a more central location near Lulu's school and bus lines.

They found an apartment three blocks from the Alamo, across from the Scottish Rite Cathedral, so downtown San Antonio became Lulu's playground and she was able to range large distances from where they lived.

In the summer, Lulu would spend many long afternoons in the air- conditioned Aztec and Majestic theaters.

Lulu wrote Betty, "You would love the lighting and decorations. It's like being in a grand palace. The Aztec has a huge pipe organ on the wall and the lights go out and you hear this loud music. Then a spotlight shines on a man playing the organ and everyone claps wildly. He plays a few minutes, then the movie begins, and I get to eat the nickel bag of popcorn I bought in the lobby. At the Majestic theater, there is a stage that just rises from below, with a big band playing wonderful swing music for a stage show. All this and a movie, sometimes a double feature, for a dime. I stay as long as I can 'cause it's so hot outside. When I was at the Aztec, last week, this creepy old man put his hand on my leg, so I moved away, but I think he followed me home, 'cause after that I saw him all the time when I went out to play. I've been having these scary dreams about him ever since. In my dreams, he opens his overcoat and is naked and he does shameful things to me. They almost seem real sometimes."

Betty quickly replied, "Gee, that's awful. You should have told the police."

"I guess you're right about the police, but that wouldn't have stopped these awful dreams," was Lulu's answer, then she changed the subject.

"I met this little black girl named Maebelle. She lives down the alley in a one-room shack with her granny, who does ironing for my Ma. I went to pick up the ironing and they asked me in to this tiny place with a big wood stove that runs on wood they have to find and chop up. Her granny irons with these strange irons. She has to heat them on that old wood stove to get them hot enough to iron with. She irons with one until it gets too cold, then she trades the cold iron for a hot one from the stove. They're solid iron, so she has to hold the handle with a thick pad. Would you believe. They have to go to the bathroom outside in an outhouse, right here in the middle of San Antonio. Both Maebelle and her granny talk kinda' funny, but they're real nice to me and told me to come visit any time, but my mom says I can't invite Maebelle to our house."

Betty answered, "I told my mom about Maebelle and she said that your mother is right. She said that black people are not the same as us and we shouldn't treat them like they are."

"Well, I don't care what either of our mothers say, I'll play with Maebelle any time I please and in her home if the weather is bad." Lulu stormed.

Within weeks, she wrote Betty again, " I have a new friend, the same age as me, Wanda Boggs. She lives about a block away in the back of her family's mattress business. We skate around the newspaper building nearby. It has wide sidewalks and grates that send up jets of cold air. Remember my gone-with-the-wind dress with the full circle skirt? Every time I skate over the grates, it flares up and Wanda's older brother and friends whistle and tease that they see my underwear. Wanda and I play in a storeroom with piles of mattresses. We hide under them and Wanda's brother tries to scare us by lying on the mattress that we're hiding under. When he does that, I feel all funny between my legs, like when Harris kissed me. Wanda says she gives herself that feeling with her hand. I tried it and It felt good, but I don't understand how. I have something else on my mind that I don't understand. I had this terrible burning down there and Mama took me to the doctor. He squirted a purple liquid where I peepee. It burned so bad I screamed. The doctor said that I had Gonorrhea and my mother has been giving me the third degree ever since. She says that some man had to do it to me before I could get that disease, but I don't remember anyone doing that except in my dreams.

Betty answered quickly, "How awful for you. I'll be glad when school is out and you can move to Austin."

Lulu replied, "Me too, but I'm afraid my dreams will go with me."

Lulu didn't tell Betty that she no longer went to the movies, or roamed about the streets as she had before, because she was afraid she would see the creepy man in the overcoat. Her fears were unfounded, because he exposed himself to the wrong person, was arrested and found guilty on numerous counts, including rape.

4

CHANGES FOR BETTY

1938

Shortly after the last time Betty and Lulu spent time together at Christmas, Betty and her sisters went back to school only to face the taunts of other children about their mother and Mr. Marshal.

Betty wrote Lulu in a letter mailed from Fredericksburg, Texas, "Julia and Vernon got married. I think she swallowed a watermelon seed. His grandpa died and his grandma is sick, so Vernon and Julia are going to take care of his grandparent's farm. His parents asked my mom to take care of the grandmother, so we all moved in to this big old house in the country on Vernon's Grandparent's farm, near Fredericksburg.

I like the school here. The kids don't know about Mr. Marshal, so we don't get teased. Mom made us bring the chickens, so I still have to take care of them, and sometimes, cows and goats. Oh well, it could be worse, they could have pigs. I can't wait to see you again. I think about you and me together kissing and I feel all funny where my peepee is, but I love it. I hope we can see each other soon. I love you, Betty."

Lulu couldn't think of how to answer Betty, so she didn't write for a while.

Betty wrote after some time had passed. "Are you mad at me? I hope not 'cause a lot is goin' on here and I need you to care.

Lulu answered immediately, "No, silly, I'm not mad at you. I just didn't know what to say about what you said about kissing me. I know I felt all funny down there, you know, when Harris kissed me, but I didn't feel that way when you kissed me, so I don't know what to say. I just want to be your best friend. "

"Alright, I'll try to stop thinking about you that way. Julia says I need to think about boys, 'cause feeling that way about girls ain't natural," Betty conceded. "So, here's what's going on here. They had to put Vernon's granny in a nursing home, so mama is out of a job . She says to not worry, 'cause Mr. Marshal has one for her. So she's moving away with him and says she'll send for us when school is out and she gets settled, but I don't know where that is and I don't want to change schools again even if I get to be with mama."

"I sure do understand how you feel about changing schools. I like the one I'm in now, but mom says that we may be moving back to Austin for the next school year. I wish my daddy would get a steady job in one place."

"Are you really going back to Austin?"

"Yes, it looks like we will move back to Austin as soon as the school year is over. My mom says that this move will last longer, 'cause it's 'a big dam job' that daddy will be working on. I hope we can move near the park where I was in the play."

"What about Christmas? Maybe I could get to Kerrville on Christmas, since Mama is there now." Betty wrote Lulu.

Lulu answered, "I don't understand about Mr. Marshal and your mom. I thought he was married."

" Mr. Marshal is married, but his wife is in a nursing home and he has this big house to take care of, so my mother is going to do that as her next job. She says that I don't have to move there if I don't want to, and I don't. So now, I get to stay here and help Julia 'til I get out of school. I want to be an animal doctor, and this

Veterinarian is letting me help him. He says he will help me get into a good school to learn to do what he does. Mary Lou and Bernice will go live with momma and she says that Mr. Marshal will help them get into college. "

"How great that you get to stay where you are and that you know what you want to be and have a way to do it. I want to be an actress, but mama says I can't make a good living that way. She says that it doesn't matter, 'cause I'll just get married and have babies anyway. Mr. Marshal sure is nice to your mom and sisters. I don't pay any attention to what my mama says about him. Sure, I hope we can see each other Christmas, but it will have to be at Aunt Vera's. My mom says I can't go to Mr. Marshal's."

Betty responded, "Well, I was right about Julia swallowing the watermelon seed. I'm glad I'm here to help. I helped the vet deliver a calf and a baby shouldn't be that different. Guess what. Mr. Marshal's wife died in the nursing home. I don't know what he'll do now. My mom said that he is going to retire soon. Hey, Christmas is just around the corner and I have a surprise for you. I'll see you then. Your ever lovin' Betty"

Christmas Surprise

Lulu was not enjoying her Christmas visit and couldn't wait for Betty to get there. She jumped every time there was a knock at the door. It was getting late and Lulu was sure the next knock would be Betty's. Lulu was disappointed when she saw that it was a boy, but he looked familiar. When he started putting one fist over another in their secret signal and mouthing 'figgy', she knew that it was Betty and they met in the middle of the room in a long hug. Lulu's cousin, Patrick chose that time to pass by and say, "We didn't say you could invite your boyfriend."

As Patrick left, Lulu stood in stunned silence. "What have I done!" She thought. "I told her I only liked to kiss boys and she's trying to be one."

Betty burst out laughing as soon as Patrick was out of earshot, then she whispered, "Fooled ya, didn't I?" And they both became overcome with laughter.

When she was able to control her laughing, Lulu said, "I thought maybe you had a cousin that looked like you." This caused another fit of laughter.

When Betty was able, she said, "I just got tired of being nagged about my unruly hair, so I had it all cut off. It still looked wild, so I had the barber put some of that stuff they put on boy's hair to keep it down and when I looked in the mirror, I realized that I looked just like a boy, so I decided to play a trick on you. Vernon loaned me these clothes."

After more giggles, Lulu said, "I knew you looked like you, but I wasn't sure til you gave our secret signals." With that, they both did the signal and said 'figgy' in unison. Nothing had changed between them. They were still best friends and they talked and laughed non-stop the rest of the visit.

After Betty left, the climate changed when Patrick reappeared and snarled, "It's enough that we treat your family every Christmas. You don't need to invite other people and make a scene." Lulu vowed that this was her last 'poor relation' visit to her Aunt's house.

When Betty got home, she wrote, "I wore Vernon's clothes for a few days and decided that I really like how they make me feel. My breasts are getting bigger and I don't like the way boys look at them. I am keeping my hair short, as it's easier to keep and I'm no longer nagged about it being messy."

What had started as a joke, slowly turned into a new direction in Betty's lifestyle.

Lulu wrote soon after the Kerrville visit, "My sister, Dorothy just told us that she is married to a man she has been dating for a while. Madison works at the University and is in the National Guard. I guess she won't be living with us anymore. Madison is real smart. He says that he's in the National Guard cause he thinks we are headed for a war. He says that a guy named Hitler in Germany is threatening to take over other countries and that we will eventually be drawn into a war. This Hitler hates Jews and Madison said that he has thugs that are breaking windows in businesses owned by Jews."

"Lulu, the way things are going in the world, both our plans might change. I don't think I ever met a Jew, but they must be smart to own businesses," Betty confessed.

"Betty Brown, you must be kidding. We went to school with lots of Jews. Rebecca Stein was in your class at school, and there were several businesses in Kerrville with Jewish owners, like Jake Rosenthal's jewelry store. My mom was always quick to point them out like they weren't as good as us, but all the Jews I know seem smarter than my mom," was Lulu's answer.

A week later, Betty wrote, "Lulu, our world is getting smaller - or bigger, depending on how you look at it. I was telling my new girlfriend, Rachel about our conversation about the Jews and she told me that her mother is Jewish and her grandparents are still in Germany. The family is real worried that they haven't heard in a long time from them. The last time they heard, the grandparents wrote about people being taken off to work camps and never heard from again. The family is afraid that they may be in one of those camps where rumor has it that they work people to death or just outright kill them. I thought our country should just stay out of things, but now, I'm not so sure."

Lulu answered immediately, "Oh, Betty, I try not to think about us going to war- for any reason. After all, Hitler hasn't attacked us. I feel awful for all the people caught up in this terrible situation, but I don't want our men to have to go over there and sacrifice their lives either."

Betty shot back, "If I was a man, I'd be the first to enlist. That crazy Hitler has to be stopped. Some day women will be allowed to go to war. I can fight as good as any guy I know."

"Betty Brown, you're talking nonsense and you know it. You are much too tender hearted to ever kill anything, certainly not another human being. I'm grateful that there are men who are willing to fight for their country, but I would never be brave enough to join them," was Lulu's reply. "Just listen to us, we never had to think about things like war when we were younger. It makes me think we were lucky to grow up in peaceful times. Seems like that luck is wearing out. No, I 'm not going to think like that. President Roosevelt pulled us out of the depression and I think he will keep us out of going to war."

A week later, Betty answers, "You put too much faith in one man, Lulu. This is a problem for the whole world. Mr. Marshal said that Hitler has invaded Poland and that if everyone just sits back, he'll gobble up the rest of Europe."

5

BACK TO AUSTIN
1939

Lulu wrote, "I was so relieved when the school year was over and we moved back to Austin. I always felt safe here, and I got my wish to live near the same park where I played the wicked queen. In fact, we found an apartment, across from the Hyde Park Baptist Church, on the same street where we lived before. It's close enough to ride my bicycle to the park.

This girl that I met at the park, when I lived here before, was coming out of church and saw me on my porch. She told me about a youth group that meets every Wednesday at the church across the street. She says that there are some really cute boys in the group, so I plan to go."

"I thought people went to church to get religion, not boyfriends, but I shouldn't talk, I know a girl named Jean. She got kicked out of her church for liking girls. They told her that it was a sin against God and she couldn't belong to the church because she told someone that she liked girls that way. I thought God wanted everybody to love one another," confessed Betty.

"I thought so too. Nothing says that you can't go to church and have a boyfriend. Is there?" asked Lulu. "I want to know more about this Jean."

Betty answered immediately, "Jean is my friend, but she'll never take your place. You will always be my best friend. Rachel is my true love, and we do it together, you know, like how Wanda told you how to pleasure yourself; Only, we do it to each other and lots more I won't mention. When you meet her, don't tell her that I told you this. She is already jealous that I talk about you all the time."

Lulu replied quickly, "No, I'd never tell Rachel that I know, 'cause that seems like something that should be kept private. I know if I ever did it with a boy, I'd strangle him if he told anyone. Let's change the subject. I went to that youth group at the church across the street. It's called Youth for Christ, or YFC. I met some nice kids, but I'm not sure I'm gonna like it. They have to memorize the books of the bible and stuff like that.

Betty waited a week to answer, "Julia had her baby and I delivered it. How's that for changing the subject? She called the doctor when her water broke, but he couldn't get there in time. I was the only one around and the baby was coming fast. I'm just glad that I knew what to do. It's a little girl and she named it after me, Jenny Lee. Bet you didn't know that my middle name is Lee, did ya? I'm thinking that I may try to be a doctor instead of a vet."

Lulu shot back, "Tell Julia congratulations, aunt Betty Lee. You'd make a great doctor. Go for it. I've got news too. I went back to that church group and a new boy, named Freddy was there. We flirted and the meeting was a little more interesting this time, so I plan to join.

A few weeks later, Betty wrote, "I hope you don't become one of those religious fanatics, ha. Well, I guess the honeymoon is over. Rachel is jealous of all the time I spend baby-sitting little Jenny Lee. Rachel doesn't know it, but I have another girlfrie. . .no, I mean lover, named Brenda. I think I like her better than Rachel."

"Betty Lee Brown, you're acting just like a man. My mom accuses my dad of 'going from titty to titty'. I wish I wasn't attracted to boys, 'cause I don't trust 'em, but I sure do like 'em, especially Freddy. He sat next to me last Wednesday and his leg brushed against mine - thrill. Oh, if I don't write for a while, it's because the church is having a revival and I'll be involved every night. The YFC has to usher and things like that. I'll get to see Freddy every night," Lulu explained.

Betty's reaction -"You sure are acting silly over that Freddy guy, but I should talk, that's just the way Rachel got my attention."

Saved

Ten days later, Lulu wrote, "Well I did it. I was saved and baptized last week. The revival was full of people from other churches and Brother Wheeler, the preacher, was really pumped up. The YFC had to stay for night church and I was really tired from ushering all day, but Freddy was there and I got to sit next to him. At the end of this long sermon about how we were all sinners and need to be saved by coming to Jesus, Brother Wheeler was shouting and turning purple in the face. I was afraid he would have a heart attack if he kept up shouting "Come to Jesus". It was really hot, and sweat was pouring off his face. Lots of people in the congregation had cardboard fans with pictures of a pale Jesus on one side of them and ads for a funeral parlor on the other, attached to sticks to hold on to. They were fanning furiously while the pianist played, 'Just as Thou Art' and Brother Wheeler pleaded, "Come - be saved now". Lots of people kept going up to the stage and holding hands, but he kept calling out for more. Next thing I knew, Freddy got up with this sappy look on his face and went up to be saved, so I followed him thinkin' if enough people went up, the sermon might be over soon and I could go home. I got to hold Freddy's hand til Brother Wheeler was satisfied and ended the sermon. I still couldn't go home 'cause all the saved sinners had to line up to shake hands with the entire congregation. Some of those little old ladies have the grip of a gorilla. One had on crochet gloves and I still had the impression of those gloves on my hand the next day. The line took forever, 'cause everyone had to say something confusin', like 'now you've been washed in the blood of the lamb'. It got me to thinkin' that I have no idea what bein' saved means.

When Betty answered, she didn't know what to say, so she asked a question. "You said you were baptized. When did that happen and what was it like? Did the sprinkle you, or dunk you?"

Lulu wrote right back. "Sorry. There was too much to tell in one letter. Well, there were so many of us 'saved souls' they couldn't use that little baptistery at the church, so we were baptized in Onion Creek. I think there must have been a hundred people watching and singing on the banks and we sinners had to wade out to the preacher in waist deep water. I wore a dress with a full skirt - big mistake. When I waded out, I had to hold my skirt down 'cause the water kept pushing it up. But when the preacher put me under the water, I had to hold my nose and my skirt went way up and I think all those people could see my underwear. I'm just glad I wore my best panties. I thought bein' saved and baptized would make me feel different, more Holy or somethin', but I don't feel a bit different except, maybe confused about what it all means.

Betty shot back, " I am so glad you confused too. You know, Mom took us to church every Sunday until those rumors about Mr Marshall went around. Then those goody-goodys treated her so bad. They're such hypocrites. They talk love but they act mean. I hope for your sake that the people in your church don't act like that. I want to believe in God. Something really huge and powerful had to make everything in the world, including us, but I think the one that church believes in is too puny to do the job."

Lulu wasted no time in answering, "Oh, I'm so glad to hear what you said, 'cause I've been having a lot of guilt about doubting Jesus and all his 'miracles'. It seems to me that a loving God wouldn't let his son be crucified for any reason and then to put the responsibility for everyone's salvation in his son's hands for eternity doesn't seem very loving. Oh, don't get me wrong, I believe there is some powerful something that I don't understand, but can count on, but I'm not sure I'm going to find that something in this church.

Betty answered quickly, "Sounds like we agree. I'm glad. Next week, I need to go visit mom. She says I shouldn't make any plans until then, so I don't know what's goin' on. I may not be writing you for a while."

"I understand. Hope you don't have to change schools. I know how you love the one you're in." wrote Lulu.

Three weeks passed before Betty answered, "You won't believe this, but the first thing Mom did when I got to Kerrville, was to take me and my sisters to Shriners and got us all new clothes, 'cause my Mom and Mr. Marshall were getting married the next day. I've never seen her so happy. The wedding was in the Baptist church where we went to church before, and lots of those kids that shamed us were there with their parents, acting like honey was melting in their mouths. My mom was beautiful in a long yellow dress and we girls wore the other colors of the rainbow. I'll send you pictures. The reception was in Mr. Marshal's, and now my mom's, big house on the hill in Kerrville. All the big shots in town were there treating us like old friends. My new girlfriend went with me and she acted like a tramp, flirting with everyone, so I dumped her. I wish I could meet a girl that likes girls but is like you, Lulu. I'm having trouble trusting anyone, but you, my Mom and sisters.

"I know what you mean about trust. So many people in my church are so goody-goody to your face, but they're just plain mean to your back. Even Brother Wheeler is two-faced. He got caught with a married lady from the choir and got kicked out of the church. But I think it's wonderful about your Mom. She deserves happiness after all she has been through. So, what does this mean for you? Are you going to move to your Mom's?" Lulu asked.

"That might be nice, living in a big house with people to wait on you, but Julia needs me here. She swallowed another watermelon seed and Vernon is slowing down. He smokes, you know. Besides, I have a great part-time job with the local vet and I want to graduate next year from the school I go to now," explained Betty. "Did I tell you that Mr. Marshal is going to send me to college if I'll go to the University with the best medical school? I don't know yet where that might be, but I hope it's in Texas."

Lulu responded, "Well, it looks like you have your future all planned. Wish I did. My folks think I should just get a job when I get out of school, like Dorothy and Jim did, so I guess I will have to work a while before I can afford to go to college. I'm going to start looking for a part-time job this week."

I've been rethinking my plans to be a doctor. That takes too long and I want to be in a position to help when war comes, and I'm sure it will. Maybe I'll train to be a nurse first."

Lulu wasted no time in answering, "Oh Betty, don't give up your dream. You would make such a good doctor. I was thinking of training to be a nurse, myself, but I'm not nearly as smart as you. "

Betty wrote by return mail, "Lulu, I'm so tired of you underrating yourself. I seem smarter to you because I'm two years older and I had a mom that told me how smart I was all the time. You never had anyone to do that for you. You are plenty smart and stop acting like you aren't. I think it would be great for us both to be nurses."

New Arrangements for Lulu - 1940

A week later, Lulu answered, "Thanks for the pep talk. I'm gonna need it, cause lots is happening. Remember I told you my sister married a man in the National guard? Well, they have a little boy now and her husband is being sent to Panama to protect the canal, so my mom and me are going to move in with Dorothy cause she works and needs help with little Tommy. It's closer to the junior high I'll be going to, so that's good. I may not have told you that the government sent my dad to Trinidad to build something for national defense, an air base, I think. It sure looks like we're getting ready to defend ourselves if we're attacked. So, I guess it's up to the women to keep the home fire's burning. Dorothy's sister-in-law, Wilda, will live with us too.

Betty waited a while to answer, "I think it's great that all the women in your family are sticking together. How many rooms do you have? Well, you'll be happy to know that I've decided to study to be a doctor after all. My mom got real upset when I told her I had decided to be a nurse and she got Mr. Marshal in on the act. I really respect him and he made a very good case for why I should study to be a doctor, including an offer to finance my college expenses for me. He wants me to call him 'dad'.

Lulu wrote back, "Good for Mr. Marshal. You'd be foolish to not take his offer. You asked about our rooms. It's a duplex and Dorothy and Wilda live in one side that has two bedrooms, and Mom and I live in the other side with one bedroom. I sleep in the living room as usual, or in the summer, I can sleep in the screened-in back porch. We're close enough to downtown to walk and my school is close too. This is good cause there's talk of gas rationing to come."

Betty took her time answering, "Remember, I told you about my girlfriend, Rachel's relatives in Germany? She's pretty sure they are dead, cause her cousin escaped

Germany and managed to get over here. He says that Hitler is trying to exterminate every Jew he can find, so many others, like Rachel's cousin, are escaping Germany and trying to find safe places to live. I think something has to be done to stop this maniac. It's good to know that we are building up our armed forces in case we are attacked. Did I tell you that Julia had a beautiful baby girl and she named her after me again, Elizabeth. That's my real name, people just call me Betty. I really love being Aunt Betty. Too bad I'll never marry, 'cause I'd love to have children.

Lulu wasted no time in answering, "Oh Betty, you're just a tomboy. You'll change your mind about men, but I won't dwell on that. Christmas is coming up. I vowed that I would never spend another Christmas at my aunt's house, but it looks like I have no choice, so I'll call you when I get there and we can plan to get together."

Betty shot back, "You don't understand about me and men. It's not as simple as being a tomboy. It's not in my mind, I feel like I am a man, but God forgot some of my equipment. I was born this way. Anyway, about Christmas, it will be so good to get together in person. This letter writing is ok, but it won't ever take the place of seeing you in the flesh."

Christmas - 1940

When Christmas came, Lulu went directly to where Betty was staying at her mother and Mr. Marshal's house. Lulu wanted to keep her vow to not spend another Christmas at her aunt's house.

When Lulu appeared at the door, Betty greeted her with, "What's wrong with your arm?" Lulu's bandaged arm was in a sling.

"Oh, I got cut and it got infected." was Lulu's answer.

"Well, come on in. I want to hear all about it." Betty indicated the living room. "Get comfortable, I'll get us a coke."

When Betty came back with the cokes, Lulu said, "Betty, you look more like a boy every time I see you."

That's 'cause I feel like a boy. You should talk, you look more like a woman every time I see you, specially your boobs."

"You're also acting more like a man." chided Lulu.

"OK, let's change the subject. How did you get cut?" asked Betty.

"Sit down and get comfortable. It's a long story." advised Lulu. Betty seated herself on the couch next to Lulu and put her coke on the coffee table in front of them, and Lulu continued. "So, I was in home room and the home room teacher, Miss Marberry, left the room. As soon as she closed the door, some boys started playing keep-away with Jeanie's purse and she started crying, so I took it on myself to try to get the purse back for her. This dumb boy, James, had it and I tried to get it from him. He pulled out this pocketknife and threatened me. I thought he was bluffing, but he wasn't. I realized that I was bleeding about the time Miss Marberry came back in. Before I knew it, the principal came in and took James away. Then an ambulance came and took me to have stitches. For no good reason, the stitches got infected a week later and had to be removed, so I'll probably have an ugly scar on my arm."

Betty interrupted, "I want to know more, but I just heard Mr. Marshal come in and I want you to meet him."

Betty went to the door and called, " Dad, could you come in here? I want you to meet Lulu."

When Mr. Marshal entered, he gave Betty a warm hug, then went to Lulu, taking her left hand, as her right hand was in a sling, he didn't wait to be introduced. "So this is the friend that Betty talks so much about. I must say, you are as pretty as she said you were. You may call me Bruce."

Lulu blushed , "Well, you are younger and better looking than she said you were and you may call me Lulu." It was Betty's turn to blush.

"Dad, Lulu was just telling me how she got cut by a boy in her home room at school."

Lulu interrupted, "He's a cedar-chopper and the stupidest boy in my class. They expelled him for cutting me."

"And what, pray tell, is a cedar-chopper?" asked Bruce.

"Oh, they're these kids that live in the country and their folks chop wood for a living. None of them are very smart.," was Lulu's answer.

"Mr. Marshal thought a minute and said, "too bad. They won't get any smarter if they don't get an education. I hope you plan to go to college like Betty here."

"I'd really like to, but my folks don't think it's important, especially for a girl. I'm going to get a job so I can save for college - at least so I can become a nurse," was Lulu's answer.

Both Betty and Lulu were surprised to hear Mr. Marshal say, "maybe I can help."

Lulu was about to speak when Bruce interrupted, "Let me explain. I always wanted to have children, but my former wife couldn't, so now it gives me great pleasure to help young people along the way. Ellen has been very generous in sharing her beautiful children with me. Even though some of them are grown, it feels like I finally have a family. Adding their friends is a special bonus to me."

"I hope that applies to my girlfriend Ruth. She's having a hard time lately and needs some good advice from someone like you." was Betty's spontaneous reaction to Mr. Marshal's offer.

"Oh, what is her problem?" asked Bruce.

"Well, you know she's Jewish and has family still in Germany, so she gets really upset when she hears about how Hitler is treating the Jews in Germany. He just made a law that all Jews have to wear a yellow star to show that they are Jewish and in Warsaw, they are putting all Jews in a ghetto, giving up their old homes and being squeezed into a small area with a wall." Betty quickly explained.

"Oh, that's terrible," gasped Lulu.

"Yes, it is," agreed Mr. Marshal, "That's why President Roosevelt has asked Congress for huge increases in preparations and mobilization training for our military and set up a General Headquarters to coordinate the effort."

"I don't understand that," said Lulu.

"It means that he's getting our country ready for war," answered Betty.

"It certainly looks that way," agreed Bruce. "They are drafting our young men for selective training and service, the first peace time draft in history. Aren't you glad you're girls?"

"I'm just so glad that we elected President Roosevelt for the third time. I trust him. He's the only president I can remember." volunteered Lulu.

"Me too," echoed Betty.

There was a lull in the conversation, so Mr. Marshal took the opportunity to get his family together to help him make a decision. "Betty, would you go up and ask your mother to join us?"

"Sure!" said Betty, and off she went.

Mr. Marshal turned to Lulu, "Lulu, I'm so pleased that you'll be staying with us."

Lulu answered enthusiastically, "Well, I want to thank you for having me, and for all the nice things you do for my best friend. Betty is so much happier since you married her mom."

"I'm the lucky one, you know, being married to such a sweet woman, who is willing to share her beautiful family with me. Not only that, Betty shares her friends with me too. Oh, here's my lovely wife now. Ellen, I was about to tell Betty and Lulu about our plans to bring mother to live with us," Mr. Marshal said, as Betty and her mother entered the room.

"I didn't know you had a mother, dad," Betty blurted.

"Silly, everyone has a mother," teased Lulu.

A flustered Betty tried to explain that she meant a mother who was alive. Then it was Lulu's turn to put her foot in her mouth, "She must be very old."

Bruce laughed and comforted Betty. "I knew what you meant dear, and yes Lulu, she is very old, ninety in fact."

Betty's mother then explained, "Betty, we wanted to consult you before we made our final decision, because it will mean the you will need to move from your nice private suite to one of our vacant rooms of your choice."

"Oh, that's perfect. I'd really prefer to have a room closer to you and Dad. I don't need all that space," Betty replied.

"Good. We need that extra room for a caregiver as my mother needs help filling her needs. She is somewhat feeble, walks with a cane, but her mind is clear as a bell," added Mr. Marshal.

"And don't worry, Lulu, this is a big house. We'll always have a room for you when you can come, and you are welcome to stay as long as you wish." added Ellen.

"Thank you so much. I may have to stay a few more days. The clinic told me that they can't put the stitches back in until the infection is all gone. Besides, I'm not too eager to go back and face all those cedar-choppers ," admitted Lulu.

Betty broke in, "Honey, you don't have to face them. You are going to miss too much school if you aren't careful. Why don't you register here in Kerrville for the next semester, which begins in two days. Your mom doesn't need you now that she lives with Dorothy and you won't have to sleep on a sofa in the living room here. You'll have your own room and we could have so much fun. I'm tired of all this letter-writing."

Lulu tried to get a word in edgewise, but Betty was so excited, she hardly took a breath. Bruce and Ellen Marshal both enthusiastically agreed with Betty that Lulu should come live with them for a while.

Lulu looked down at the carpet and slowly traced it's pattern with her foot. "I don't know what to say. I think I need to talk to my mom and think about it for a while."

"You do that, dear, and take your time. Just know that you are most welcome here as long as you wish to stay. Now, I think we old folks need to hit the hay as they say in some circles." said Ellen as she gave Lulu, then Betty, a hug.

Bruce gave both girls a warm hug and agreed with everything Ellen had said.

When they got to their room, Ellen put her arms around Bruce and asked, "Did I do the right thing? You know things can get pretty lively when those two girls get together.

Kerrville - February, 1941

Lulu moved into the Marshal's in time to register for the new semester in Kerrville. She and Betty were doing their homework together in Lulu's room.

" Did you have this much homework in Austin?" Betty asked.

"No, but it was harder," answered Lulu. "I love everything in my Kerrville classes better than in Austin - including more homework. I'm so glad you talked me into coming here. I've never had as much fun as I've had with you and Grammy this last month. It's hard to believe that she's ninety years old."

"Yeah, she has more energy than you and me put together." agreed Betty. "She's had another one of her wild brainstorms and wants us to come out to her apartment when we finish our homework. I'm finished"

"I'm tired of doing this, so let's go now," Lulu said this as she tossed her homework into her book bag.

As the two girls walked briskly toward Grammy's suite, Lulu questioned Betty. "What's going on with you and your girlfriend, Rachel? I haven't heard you mention her in days."

"I'll make a deal with you. I won't talk about her if you'll stop yammering about all those cute boys in your class." Betty tossed this over her shoulder and increased her pace.

Lulu was having to run to keep up with Betty, but she panted, "I was just asking a friendly question."

Betty stopped and turned to Lulu, "Look, I know you mean well, but I can't talk about it just yet. Maybe later."

"Sure, Betty. I didn't mean to upset you." Lulu replied.

By now, the girls are at Grammy's door and Betty suggests, "Let's pretend this conversation didn't happen and let's go in and have a great time with Grammy."

"Gotcha!", says Lulu as she knocks on the door.

Grammy's voice is heard, "Come on in, I'm on the phone."

As the girls enter, Lulu gazes around the room, gasps and whispers to Betty, "I can't believe it. She's made it even weirder."

To their right, hangs a shark's jaw with a Barbie doll in it's teeth, and to the left is a skull with a rose in its mouth. There are Mardi Gras beads everywhere accented by various eccentricities, such as voodoo masks and such - not exactly what one would expect to see in the living room of a ninety-year-old.

As the girls take it all in, Grammy's voice is heard as she talks on the phone. "Of course, Eleanor, I'd love to have Lenore stay here as long as you need for the conference. She can catch me up on your latest passionate cause. ...You know that she's one of my favorite young friends. ...Do you need my son to send a car for her?...Then I'll expect her soon. Bye for now."

As she ends the conversation, Lulu and Betty seat themselves in comfortable chairs opposite the couch where Grammy, who looks more like sixty than ninety, sits.

" Great. We're going to have company. My good friend, Eleanor, is attending a YWCA conference in Fredericksburg and needs a place for her daughter, Lenore, to stay til it's over, so she'll drop her by here later today, on her way to the conference. Lenore is your age,

Lulu, a little wild, but smart as a whip. Lenore's father is president of the University in Austin, but I understand that he is having problems with the board of regents, because he is defending some young professors who are pushing for integration."

Lulu asked in all seriousness, "integrating what?"

Betty laughed, "Lulu, those professors want to pass a law so black kids can go to the same schools we do."

A crestfallen Lulu merely said, "oh."

Grammy to the rescue, "I'll bet Lulu doesn't know any black people."

"No," Lulu answered, "except the people who work here for Mr. Marshal. Oh, but I used to play with a little black girl when I lived in San Antonio. She and her granny lived down the alley from us and they always welcomed me into their one little shack, but mom wouldn't let me ask Maebelle into our house. Oh, and I remember that I did know one black man when I was real little. He worked for my aunt at her cleaning business. He was so much fun - always cheerful even though most people, when they spoke to him, used that 'n' word with his name, Jim, but he didn't seem to mind."

"Oh, he minded being called 'nigger Jim' alright, but he needed the job." was Grammy's wry retort.

"How do you girls feel about sharing our schools with black folks?"

Still reeling from hearing Grammy utter the 'n' word, Betty showed her discomfort at the question by squirming in her chair and buttoning her shirt. Lulu fooled with her hair as she always did when confronted with a problem she couldn't solve. They were both relieved when there was a knock on the door.

"That couldn't be Lenore so soon," Grammy mumbled as she moved to the door, but when she opened it, the girls saw another girl, about their age, but quite different in appearance. The stylish suit she wore looked like it came out of the latest issue of a fashion magazine. Soft brown curls framed a heart-shaped face with full lips, a cute turned-up nose, and large blue eyes. As the door opened, she spread her arms, bowed slightly and confidently belted out a theatrical, 'TA-DA'.

Grammy grinned , "Well, now that you've made your entrance, come in and meet my new friends, Betty and Lulu."

After introducing Lenore to the girls, Grammy remarked, " I thought Eleanor would come in for a while."

"Oh, mother said that she would visit with you when she picks me up. She was in a big hurry, because she's on the YWCA board and needed to get some things done before the conference started. This is a national conference, you know. I can't imagine why they held it in tiny Fredericksburg. Mrs. Marshal, I've been on the road too long. I need to pee." said Lenore without taking a breath.

Lulu gasped and Betty couldn't believe her ears. It was considered vulgar in 1940, to say why you were being excused, but Grammy didn't blink. "Of course dear, right through that door."

As soon as the door closed, Betty observed, "She certainly is sure of herself, isn't she." Lulu agreed.

"That confidence comes from her traveling a great deal, being treated as an equal by her intelligent parents, and mingling with highly educated people. She's just a young girl at heart, like you and Lulu. Give her a chance. You'll see. She's had advantages your parents couldn't give you." Grammy tried to explain.

Lenore burst in saying, "Whew, my bladder thanks you. Now, where were we? Lulu and Betty giggled.

"Just before you arrived, the girls and I were discussing integration and I had just asked them how they felt about going to school with black children." Grammy explained.

Lenore was vehement, "That's a no-brainer. It's absolutely uncivilized that Negroes in this country pay taxes, can vote, and do most of the hard work, but their children aren't allowed to go to the school of their choice like white children can. I went to school in France and people of color were in my classes. They're just as smart as we are when they can get a good education."

Betty and Lulu were impressed by Lenore's passion, as was Grammy, who questioned. "Is it true that your father shares your views, Lenore?"

"Oh yes, and mother too. She has been lobbying to get the YWCA integrated ever since she joined the board. Dad is having some problems with the board of Regents, because he is supporting some liberal professors who are pushing for equality in the schools. So it's a family view. My sister, Helen, feels the same." was Lenore's self-assured answer.

Grammy turned to Betty, "We haven't heard your views on the subject, dear. What say you?"

Betty squirmed a bit before answering, "You know, I have never known any black people, until I moved here and met the cook, the maids and the chauffer. They lived way on the other side of town and couldn't go to restaurants or places like that where I went, so I only saw them at a distance. I really never thought about us going to school together."

"Lulu, you told us earlier that you knew two people of color when you were much younger. What would you think about going to school with them?" queried Grammy.

"Well, Jim would be too old to go to school with me." ventured Lulu. Betty and Lenore giggled, but Lulu didn't see what she'd said that was funny. "Any way, I wouldn't mind going to school with Maebell. She was fun, but she'd have a lot of catching up to do. Her English was awful."

"I guess it's my turn to give an opinion on the subject. I think it's disgraceful that our country sent colored men to fight and die in World War I, but won't allow their children have the advantage of better schooling." was Grammy's contribution. "Now that we know each other better, let's play a bit. I asked Betty and Lulu here today to show them a fun game I have discovered. I'm glad you can join us, Lenore."

Lenore was quick to respond, "Count me in. I love games." Betty and Lulu agreed.

Grammy continued, "It started because I have to get up at night to go to the bathroom and I have knees that are bone-on-bone and they hurt even more at night than usual. Well, I learned in psychology books, that the mind has difficulty focusing on two things at once, so I decided to distract my brain when I had to get up, by telling myself stories. To get started, I decided to try to make up stories where all the words start with the same letter, like - 'Alice acted anxious at auctions,' etc.

The girls tittered and Lenore volunteered, "How about, Bouncy Betty belched like a boy?"

To which, Betty countered, "loudmouth Lenny, left, licking her lumps."

Then Lulu chimed in, "Both bad babes better behave."

"Yes, girls are going to get along, or Grammy will get grumpy." Grammy added and everyone laughed. Lenore and Betty hugged and peace was restored.

"This is fun. Let's do some more," Lulu suggested.

"I'm so glad you enjoyed it, because I had more in mind. I thought we could have a contest each week to make the best story with a letter, starting with 'A', Then we could include the winners in a little book we could donate to some charity. We might even include some of the better runner ups." Grammy proposed.

The girls all agreed that this was a great idea, but Lenore moaned, "But I won't be here to compete."

Lulu responded quickly, "Sure you can. You can mail your entry in."

The girls went into a huddle, sharing their enthusiasm for the project, but Grammy sat down, saying, "Ladies, I fear that I am fading. You are welcome to continue, but I still have my spiritual work to do, and I am getting weary. Lenore, I wanted to visit with your mother. Since it is getting late, and you have a long drive ahead of you, I'm sure you can persuade her to stay over, so we can visit at breakfast. The guest room is right next to my bedroom and has twin beds, so you should be comfortable. Betty, please let them know in the kitchen that I would like breakfast for two in my room at eight. You girls can make any arrangements for breakfast that you wish. Now, let's have some hugs, so I can absorb some of your youthful energy." Grammy hugged each girl warmly, wishing each girl well, while trite phrases like, 'sleep tight. Don't let the bedbugs bite', were exchanged.

As the door closed, and the girls started back to the living room, Lenore noted, "I can't believe she's ninety. My grandmother is in her seventies and she looks and acts older than Grammy."

"Yeah, and she's more fun than most of the kids I know," piped in Lulu.

Betty chimed in, "I like the idea of a contest of same-letter stories."

"Me too," said Lenore. "In fact, I thought of a great beginning for one, but it starts with 'F'."

"That's alright, we could make up a group story and surprise Grammy. What's the beginning?" asked Betty.

" The only thing is that it's a little off-color." admitted Lenore.

"Even better," laughed Lulu, and Betty agreed.

"OK, here goes, Freddy's father farted fiercely in front of friends." Lenore giggled. She was joined in laughter by the others.

Their laughter was interrupted by a knock on the door. "I'll get it. It's probably my mother," said Lenore, still laughing.

The Next Morning

Grammy and Eleanor are having breakfast in Grammy's living room and have been having a lively conversation bringing each other up-to-date on her life.

Eleanor was saying, "It's so unfortunate, but the board felt that we had no choice but to prepare as though a war is inevitable. No one wants it, but we have been told that there is a very real possibility that war is coming."

Grammy's thoughtful response was, "Well, I suppose we should be prepared for war, but I'm sure that President Roosevelt will do everything in his power to avoid one. But tell me about the rumors I hear that Homer is having trouble with the Board of Regents?"

"You heard right. You know my husband. He'll always stand up for people when he feels that they are right. The Board of Regents have insisted that he fire several young firebrand professors, who are advocating changes in policy. Homer feels that they have valid reasons for their opinions, especially one who is very vocal about integrating blacks into our schools. Right now, it's a stand-off, but the board has the power to fire him and they threaten to do just that."

"If they do, he should run for governor and fire the entire board," was Grammy's firm opinion.

There was a knock on the door and the girls burst in as soon as they heard Grammy say 'come in', and gave hugs all around. The energy in the room was palpable.

"You girls seem super-charged. What's going on?" asked Grammy.

They all started to speak at once and were finally able to let their elders know that they had collaborated on a same-letter story in anticipation of the contest. Then, they had to explain the contest and it's origin to Eleanor, who said, "I can't wait to hear this."

"I think we should have some introductions first. Eleanor, you have not met Betty and Lulu, you know," interrupted Grammy.

"It's very nice to meet you both. It looks like my daughter has made two new friends. I can't wait to hear your story." offered Eleanor.

Betty began, "OK, here goes. Freddy's father feasted on fried frijoles, filling him with flatulence."

Lenore continued, "on Friday, he farted in front of Freddy's friends, Fay and Frank."

Lulu concluded, "Frank fled. Fay fainted and fell flat on the floor, and Freddy fanned the fecal fumes furiously.

Amid much clapping and laughter, the girls all bowed and collapsed on the couch.

Eleanor reluctantly stated, "you seem to be having so much fun. I hate to have to take Lenore away, but she has school tomorrow." The girls expressed their disappointment, so she added, "don't worry, I'll bring her back the next time we have a break."

As Lenore and her mother prepared to leave, the girls exchanged addresses and phone numbers amid urging each other to keep in touch. When the door closed, those remaining felt as though the air had been sucked from the room. Betty and Lulu collapsed on the couch as Grammy tidied up. She finally broke the silence, "It was so good to visit with my old friend again, but she had some disturbing information. It seems that our government feels that we are close to being in a war and has encouraged the YWCA to prepare for that possibility."

"Getting ready, doesn't mean it's going to happen," piped Lulu.

"Right. President Roosevelt is too smart for that to happen." added Betty.

"I hope you're right," was Grammy's low-key comment. "Now, I hope you girls will excuse me. I have a busy day ahead of me and I need to get ready."

After Grammy leaves, there is a long silence, which is finally broken by Betty, "I'm sorry I cut you off about Rachel earlier. I just couldn't talk about it then, but I'll try now."

"That's alright. It's none of my business anyway." Lulu interrupted.

"It certainly is your business. I broke up with her because of you. I realized that I didn't love her like I love you. I didn't want to be with her all the time, or want to take care of her, like I do you." As the words poured out of Betty, she put her arms around Lulu,

"Please Betty. You know I can't give you the kind of love you want. I love you as a dear best friend. That's all." Lulu pleaded as she pushed Betty away.

"Please Lulu. How do you know if you haven't tried it. Let me teach you. I can give you all the pleasure that a man can. I just can't give you babies." As Betty poured out these words, she was trying to put her arms around Lulu again, but Lulu resisted, loudly pleading, "Leave me alone!"

Betty turned to go, bumping into a small table and toppling a vase to the floor. As she slammed the door, Grammy emerged from her bedroom, asking "What's going on in here?"

Lulu collapsed on the couch, crying. Grammy sat down next to her and tried to comfort her. "There, there, tell Grammy what's bothering you. Did you and Betty have an argument?"

Lulu nodded and tearfully added, "oh, Grammy, I think I just lost my best friend."

"Nonsense child, a friendship like yours won't be lost with one argument. Give it time. You'll see." Grammy put her arm around Lulu and told her stories of friendships she had thought she had lost, but hadn't, and finally, Lulu stopped crying.

6

MENDING FENCES

Grammy was right, of course. Lulu and Betty both apologized to the other, and their relationship gradually went on as though nothing had happened. Betty let Lulu know that she would no longer have any expectations that Lulu would be more than her best friend. A few weeks after the argument, Betty resumed her relationship with Rachel.

The girls had three more months of school before summer break. As the weeks past, the household settled into a predictable pattern. Weekdays, everyone had different schedules, so breakfast and lunch varied for each member, but the evening meal was always at the same time and everyone was expected to attend, unless they had another engagement.

Conversation at dinner was lively and shared by all. Ellen Marshal kept everyone informed about Betty's sisters.

Julia, the oldest, now had two children and was helping her husband, Vernon, take care of his family's farm. Bernice, who was a senior in high school, lived with them and helped with the children. Geraldine and Mary Lou were away in college.

Lulu kept the group abreast of her family in Austin as she corresponded with them regularly. Her mother took care of her sister's little boy, while her sister, Dorothy, worked. Dorothy's husband, who was still in Panama with the National Guard, reported that the forces there were preparing for the event of war.

The girls were so busy with school and the contest that they hardly noticed how the nation was moving ever closer to war. Mr. Marshal pointed out that the threat was no longer just in Europe, but a new danger had appeared in the Pacific as Japan became belligerent toward the United States, because of it's aid to China.

The routine was broken by the playing of Grammy's same letter contest. Each week, the three girls submitted their version of a story told by using words beginning with the same letter. Grammy judged which was the best and the next week, they went on to the next letter in the alphabet.

Lenore, who mailed her submission from Austin, won for the letter 'A'. She set a slightly racy tone with the following: "Ambitious Alice acting antsy and airing her ass-ets for all to admire as she aimed at adding an amorous addition to her already abundant achievers, asking at all assemblages she attended. Are there any attendees aiming at an affair? I am available."

Conversation was not always so much fun. Lulu and Betty were getting an education from listening to Grammy and her son debate the possibility of war.

"I can't believe I reared a son who would praise war, " Grammy was saying one night as Lulu and Betty came to dinner.

"Mother, I was merely pointing out that we have wars because there are so many who benefit from them," Mr. Marshal answered.

"I don't understand that, dad," Betty interjected.

"Well, besides the obvious benefactors, the arms dealers and the munitions manufacturers, there are all the citizens who were previously out of work. A war build-up brings full employment and prosperity." was Mr. Marshal's response.

Grammy's passionate response was, "I don't care how many people profit from war. It's evil, and I will fight against it til my dying breath. There are too many warmongers out there. The world needs more Peacemongers, like me."

"I'm with you Grammy. I'm a Peacemonger." Lulu agreed.

"Well, I'm a Peacemonger too, but so far that hasn't changed the direction we're going. Just yesterday, President Roosevelt signed the Lend-Lease bill. It says that our country will supply arms to England and China and allow them to pay us later." Mr. Marshal explained.

"Boy, that ought to make Hitler mad," cited Betty.

"And how about Hirohito?" Grammy countered.

"Who?" asked Lulu.

"The emperor of Japan, dear, " explained Grammy. Lulu looked puzzled, so Grammy added, "Japan and China are at war, so helping China, would make Japan's emperor angry."

"You can put me down as a Peacemonger, Grammy. I lost my first husband to a war and had to raise my four girls by myself. Betty never knew her father." Mrs. Marshal volunteered.

"No, but I have a great dad now that I'm almost grown." added Betty as she gave Mr. Marshal a hug.

February and March, 1941

February and March settled into a sameness on week days for Betty and Lulu. School, homework, once a week, a same-letter contest, and a group dinner every night.

One event threatened the peaceful pattern. In late March, Lulu asked Jerry, a boy from her class, to dinner. During the meal, Betty scowled at Jerry and said, "I can't see what Lulu could possibly see in you." At the end of the meal, Betty went abruptly to her room.

When Lulu's guest left, she knocked on Betty's door. As soon as Betty opened the door, Lulu questioned, "What was that all about? I thought we had an understanding about our relationship. How would you like it if I was rude to Rachel?"

"I wouldn't mind a bit. It would mean that you were jealous. My God, does that mean that you're sleeping with that boy?" demanded Betty.

"No, but I like him a lot and you have no right to be jealous. I've made it very clear that my feelings for you are those of a best friend, and I'm having trouble feeling friendly when you act like this." was Lulu's adamant answer as she left the room.

Lulu didn't speak to Betty for almost a week, when Betty apologized and promised to try to do better. After that, their relationship slowly returned to being a close friendship.

The same-letter contest was held every Friday night. So far, Lenore and Betty had won twice and Lulu had won three times. The second week in April, the same letter contest was for the letter 'H'. Lenore and Lulu tied, so both of their sentences were read at dinner.

"Heavenly Heather, helping herself and her heirs with her huge heart.

Holding her honor high, she humbly helps heal hearts in hospice home," was Lenore's entry.

Betty's entry was slightly risque. "Handsome Hal, hoping his huge hanky hump will hide his humble hanging."

7

WEEKENDS

Saturdays everyone was free to plan their own schedules, and Sunday, everyone was expected to go to church.

Grammy, however, announced that her God was too vast to fit into a church and that she would be staying at home on Sundays, communicating with the God of her understanding.

Her son was quick to come to her defense. "I thought you might say that, Mother, and if I was single, that would be my preference. That's the way you raised me, but I have a family to think of now and we will attend the church of my wife's choice."

Lulu spoke up, "I would like to stay at home with Grammy on Sundays. Maybe she can help me find some answers. I certainly didn't find them in the church I used to go to. My parents won't mind. They don't go to church either."

Grammy was obviously pleased, "Lulu, I would love to spend time with you exploring our Spiritual paths. It's a lifetime journey, you know. Let's have breakfast together next Sunday and we can discuss it."

Lulu gratefully agreed. "Just name the time and place."

"Let's say in my room at nine. I like to sleep in on Sundays. I'll have breakfast sent in."

Lulu knocked on Grammy's door at the stroke of nine and entered when she heard Grammy saying, "come in dear". As they began their breakfast, Grammy said that she had a question for Lulu, and Lulu answered that she had a question for Grammy.

Grammy said, "Well they say that age comes before beauty, so here is my question. I want to know all about your earlier experience in a church that you spoke of."

Lulu related how she went forth to be 'saved' because of a cute boy, and how she was baptized in a creek and her dress floated up showing her underwear, and how she did not really believe that Jesus was the son of God, or that he could wash away your sins, and finally how disappointed she had become in the preacher and many of the congregation.

When she finished her long discourse, she asked Grammy, "Now, what did you mean when you said that your God was too vast to fit into a church?"

Grammy chuckled and took a minute before she answered, "I guess I should have added, a temple, a mosque, a tabernacle, or any other place where people worship a God of their understanding. I call my God, Creator, and anything that can create a Universe is too large to fit into any building or belief system. When I was in my seventies, I wrote a poem that tells my beliefs better than I can today. Do you want to hear it?"

Lulu responded that she did, so Grammy went to get a copy. "I used to memorize my poetry, but I don't trust my memory at this late date, so I'll read it to you."

8

CONCESSION

The artist and poet ponder God, argue and dissect.
Poet can't trust theories filtered through cold intellect.
Atheist scorns Spiritual passion from a Poet's heart.
Could both share elements of truth if they just reflect?
Perhaps in science there's wisdom neither will reject.

Let's concede, 'Big Bang' and "Let There Be Light"
could have been the same event and end our plight.
If true, we each must accept the other's premise.
If I'd embrace your thought with intellectual delight,
You'd acknowledge less spite, more spiritual might.

I create a God to meet my hungry need - I concede.
It is energy, atoms, skin, bones, and blood we bleed.
Supersoul, weaving light through warp and weft of all.
Spirit without gender, allowing men to plant their seed,
But trusting only woman to keep the Peace and breed.

My concession is covered with landmines of fear.
I cling to benign Deity when dark thoughts appear,
don't want to face evil and Good as one fiery force.
I seek a loving God like that New Testament Dear.
Not Old Book Terminator wearing his warlike gear.

You can't concede a God who'd allow a Holocaust.
My God must be Omnipotent else my theory's lost.
I must concede God's dark side, though it terrifies,
So, I'll acknowledge that dark and light are crossed,
If you will cede our Universe wasn't blindly tossed.

Great minds in both science and theology disagree.
Niels Bohr has a theory which we both might see,
"The opposite of a profound truth is also profound."
Scientists grow closer to whether or what God be.
Til then let's swim together in a slightly skeptical sea.

There was a long silence while Lulu tried to find words for what she felt. "Grammy, I am in awe of all of your talents. I can tell that this is a great poem. What I would like to ask you is about the part where you see your God as a Spirit or super-soul, not like I do, as an old man with a beard."

"Yes, I don't have a clue as to what God looks like, but the God of my understanding has many qualities that define it, such as, Energy, Love, Intelligence, creativity, including all of nature, lack of fear, lack of gender, and more that I can't think of at the moment." was Grammy's reply.

"Gosh, that's a lot to try to wrap my brain around. I want to think about that for a while, then I have some more questions. I need to get ready to meet Jerry. We're going for a log walk down by the river. He doesn't go to church either and I'll bet he'll have something to say about your poem. Could I have a copy to show him?"

"Of course, dear. Take this copy, I have more. Say hello to Jerry for me."

"I will. Hope you have a good rest of the day," Lulu said as she turned to leave.

Unfortunately, that did not happen. As Lulu was leaving, Grammy stood to go to the bathroom, took a few steps, and fell. When Lulu saw Grammy on the floor, she had a moment of indecision, then threw open the door and called, "Help, Grammy's fallen." She then rushed to Grammy's side and took her hand. "Oh, Grammy, please be alright, please open your eyes." Grammy obliged, but they had a glazed look in them.

Mr. Marshal and Betty rushed in as they had been down the hall when Lulu called. Bruce immediately took charge. "Let's move her to her bed," he said.

"No, dad, she may be injured. Let me examine her to see." interrupted Betty as she knelt beside Grammy. Lulu joined her and they examined Grammy for injuries. She was conscious and able to respond to questions, so the girls soon determined that she was not injured. Grammy kept repeating, "I couldn't feel my feet touch the floor and I lost my balance."

"Her neuropathy has advanced. Doctor Tate said that this would happen." said Bruce as he knelt beside Grammy.

"Mother, the girls think that you are not injured, but I'd feel better if we got the doctor to take a look at you before we move you." he said as he held Grammy's hand. Grammy nodded.

Fortunately, the doctor lived nearby and was at home. Dr. Tate quickly determined that the girls were right in their appraisal of Grammy's condition. He praised them for their quick thinking in not moving Grammy and told them he might have jobs for them if they decided to pursue medicine as a career. He got Grammy into bed, gave her a sedative and said goodnight. Both Betty and Lulu decided that they would spend the night in Grammy's apartment just to be sure she didn't fall again.

Mr. Marshal realized that some changes had to be made, so, when Grammy had recovered from the shock of falling, a family conference was called so that everyone's ideas could be heard.

9

FAMILY CONFERENCE

When the time came for the family to meet, Grammy was still napping. When everyone else settled into Grammy's living room, Mr. Marshal started the ball rolling. "Thank you all for coming. We need to talk about how we can assure my mother's safety. I, personally think that someone should always be in attendance when she needs to move around. Her peripheral neuropathy has progressed to the point that she doesn't have feeling in her feet and it's going to get worse. The cells are dying and it is moving up her legs. She can't find her balance, so she should not be trying to walk. "

Lulu added, "she said that her knees hurt. I thought she just had arthritis."

"I'm afraid it's both, but neuropathy is far more serious and non-reversible," was Bruce's answer.

Grammy's bedroom door opened and an attendant pushed Grammy in her wheelchair into the meeting. "I'm so sorry to be late. I hope you started without me," apologized Grammy.

"Think nothing of it, mother. I was just explaining that you would need someone at your call at all times," said her son.

Grammy interrupted, "As much as I don't like that idea, I can see the wisdom in it. I want you all to know that I will not be like my husband, who fought any loss of his independence. I know that you all care as much for me as I care for you all and you have my best interests at heart."

Ellen was quick to answer, "We certainly do, Grammy. Bruce is making sure that any time you need someone to help you, they'll be there. My husband and I, and several on our staff, will be available at all times."

Betty stood up to be recognized, "Lulu and I have been talking and we want to take turns staying with Grammy at night, so she can just tell us when she needs help."

Lulu interrupted, "You know, Betty wants to be a doctor and I want to be a nurse, and this would be good training for us. Besides, we both enjoy being with you, Grammy."

"And you both know how much I love being with you both. So, it sounds as though we have a plan. When do we start?" Grammy asked the group.

Mr. Marshal answered, "It looks like we've already started, so I suggest that it's time to adjourn."

As the rest were getting things together to leave, Betty and Lulu were whispering to each other. Then, Betty spoke up, "If it's alright, Lulu and I want to stay with Grammy a while before we leave."

"Oh, I was hoping you would. Maybe we can play a game." enthused Grammy.

The rest of the family said their goodnights with a lighter heart than they had at the beginning of the meeting. When the last one left, Betty turned to Grammy, "you know Grammy, Lulu and I were wondering about what you said about your late husband. You've never talked about him. We were hoping you'd tell us about what you meant."

"Oh dear, I was afraid to mention him, because I really don't want to relive those years, but now that I have aroused your curiosity, I'll only say that I feel that

I owe my deceased husband for being my teacher. He taught me patience, as he could be somewhat difficult, and the most valuable lesson of all, that I had to live my life in love, not fear. I had to be patient to survive his constant negativity. Watching him live out the end of his life in fear, showed me that I needed to find a better way to live - in love. I'll tell you more some time, but let's just have fun tonight." The rest of the evening was filled with laughter as they played a game in which they each tried to find the silliest way to throw the dice, and where anyone who won, screamed and levity was the theme of the evening.

April, 1941

The residents of Marshal Manor settled into a routine on weekdays in April. Betty and Lulu had school, then homework, then dinner with the family. They took turns staying with Grammy at night.

In addition to cheery talk of the events of everyone's day, dinner conversation always included the imminent danger of war with Germany; but in March the focus began to shift to the possibility of war with Japan. Mr. Marshal pointed out that Japan could not continue its war with China if the US didn't lift embargoes it had placed on trading gasoline, iron, steel and other items necessary for Japan to wage a war. He felt that Japan would retaliate for these embargoes. The gravity of the world situation often sent the family to bed with a dire sense of foreboding.

Weekends varied a bit, as everyone was free to spend it as they wished. Saturdays, Bruce and Ellen usually visited with friends or attended to business.

Lulu had a standing date with Jerry. Sometimes they took in a movie, but most often, they went for long walks and talked. Grammy's poem had put them both on a spiritual path that they were both eager to explore.

Betty spent some time with Rachel, but since they had few interests in common, other than sex, Betty spent most of Saturday with Grammy. This was fortunate for Grammy as she found it difficult to leave her apartment, and for Betty who absorbed Grammy's wisdom, like a sponge.

Sundays, the Marshals took Betty to church with them, and Lulu got to be the sponge for Grammy's wealth of wisdom. She didn't want to forget a thing she was learning in her talks with Jerry and Grammy, so she began to write a journal of her spiritual journey.

ENTRY ONE - *Lulu's Spiritual Journal*

"My first exposure to religion was when I was about five and went to Sunday school with neighbors. As best as I can remember, I thought Jesus was God, who would punish me if I was not good and doom me to Hell, a really awful place, when I died. We moved and I didn't go to church again for years, but I always felt guilty on Sunday if I didn't go to church.

When I entered my teens, I moved again to Austin, across the street from the Hyde Park Baptist Church. I joined a youth group there and my idea of God began to change from 'God Jesus' to 'Jesus, the son of God. I knew what they both looked like, because I'd seen pictures of this old, bearded God and his pale, long-haired son, Jesus. There was a lot of talk about the Holy Spirit, but no pictures, so I didn't quite figure where that fit in.

I couldn't believe the idea that we are all sinners, or that God let Jesus die to save us from those sins. I became disillusioned with that church and stopped going to any church when I moved away."

Later that day, Betty came by and was complaining about having to go to church with her parents every Sunday, so Lulu let her read what she had written in her journal.

When she finished reading, Betty said. "Gee, Lulu, you surprise me. As long as I've known you, I didn't know that you thought so much about God."

"And I'm surprised that we haven't talked about it that much. What do you think God is?" asked Lulu.

"I don't think much about it. I don't want to go to church with my folks, but I don't want them to be disappointed in me." answered Betty.

"That doesn't answer my question," said Lulu.

"I guess I just take everything they say about God in church as the truth, but it makes me feel bad about myself, because I do so many things the church says are evil. I guess I'll just go to Hell when I die, because I can't stop loving other girls."

"Betty, I thought you were smarter than that. Don't you know that you have a choice about the kind of God you believe in? I realized that when I read Grammy's poem. I want you to read it. It'll start you thinking for yourself." suggested Lulu as she picked up the poem. "Oh, I only have this copy. I'll read it to you."

As Lulu read, she had new insights. When she finished, both she and Betty were quiet for a bit, each in deep thought. Finally, Betty asked if she could take the poem if she promised to make a copy for Lulu and Lulu agreed as she was already writing her next journal entry in her mind.

ENTRY TWO - *Lulu's Spiritual Journal*

Lately, I've been thinking that God is probably more at home in nature than in a church. The biggest change in my thinking has come from Grammy's poem that says that scientists might know more about God than preachers do. Jerry, who is studying physics, says that everything in the universe is made up of atoms and we are all connected - even to a God that created everything. Somehow, this makes sense to me. I'm starting to believe that God is an invisible 'IT', like energy or intelligence. This is a lot to think about. I'll try to journal more as I understand more."

This was the first of many conversations between Betty and Lulu about religion and spirituality. Gradually, the rift in their relationship started to mend as their understandings grew.

May, 1941

As summer approached, tension began to build for both Betty and Lulu. Lulu was in her room crying as she read a letter, when Betty knocked and burst in without waiting for Lulu to respond. Lulu quickly turned her head to hide her tears, but Betty didn't notice as she had other things on her mind.

"Hey Lulu, I need some advice. Doctor Tate just offered me a summer job, but dad has set up a bunch of visits to colleges he wants us to look at. I want to do both, but I don't know how to make that happen. What would you do?

Lulu wiped away her tears and answered, "I dunno."

"You've been crying. What's the matter honey?" Betty asked.

"My mom says I gotta help her take care of my nephew this summer, 'cause she's taking a summer job at the bakery." said Lulu as she showed Betty the letter. "With you being so busy and me being gone, who's going to help Grammy at night? And once I'm gone, I won't have an excuse to come back, and I really like being here with you and your family, and Jerry - and I love the school here. Oh, Betty, what am I going to do?"

It was Betty's turn to say, 'I dunno', but as they discussed their situations, they decided to bring them up that night at family dinner.

When dinner time came, everyone except Mr. Marshal was seated, but it was customary for everyone to be present before Grace was said, so they waited. Soon he stormed in growling, "Those damn Germans just sank one of our freighters in the South Atlantic. Surely Roosevelt will declare war now."

Grammy expressed the feelings of the rest of the group, "Oh, I hope he doesn't. Surely there are other diplomatic measures that could be taken."

Ellen saw an argument coming and, ever the diplomat, she said, "I guess we can't solve that one here, but I'll bet someone here has another problem we can talk about."

"I guess that would be me," volunteered Betty. "Doctor Tate just offered me a job for the summer and dad has made plans for us to visit some colleges. I want to do both, but don't know where to start trying to change plans we've already made."

"That's an easy fix. Just work out a schedule with the doctor and we can work around it. He doesn't work on weekends, so we could go then." said Bruce.

Betty said, "Great, and Lulu has a problem too. She doesn't want to change schools after the summer."

"It's more than that. I feel like I'll be letting Grammy down and I'll miss everyone so much and I've changed schools so often." Lulu said all this while fighting back her tears.

"Well, you can stop worrying about changing schools. I have been planning to write your mother asking if you could live with us during the school year until you graduate. I'll do that right away." said Mr. Marshal.

"I'll miss you in the summer, but please don't feel that you have failed me in any way. You've been a source of joy since I've known you." said Grammy.

Betty stepped in, "I'll miss you like crazy, but we can write like we used to, and Austin is not that far. Maybe we could visit on weekends."

Lulu felt a lot better, but what she couldn't say was that she would miss her time with Jerry most. She was beginning to feel closer to him than she had ever felt toward anyone else.

Ellen joined in, "It's not like you won't have friends there. Lenore will be happy to spend time with you."

"Oh, and speaking of Lenore, she won the same letter contest this week. Can you believe that we're on the letter 'n'?" said Grammy.

"Let's hear the winner," urged Bruce.

Grammy shuffled through her papers and found the winner, "Here goes - Nervous Nellie never knew the niceties of nature until Nathan nudged her to navigate native Navaho knowledge. Now Nellie knows, 'nature is nicer'."

There was general applause, then Lulu said, "I'm going to write her to congratulate her and tell her to get ready for a good time this summer."

Betty left after dinner, feeling much happier about summer plans, but Lulu was still wrestling with her feelings for Jerry and decided to stay and talk to Grammy about it.

When they got comfortable, Grammy asked Lulu, "What's the problem?"

"You know, I told you before how much I enjoyed the long talks I had with Jerry. Well lately, he's not that interested in talking. Ever since he kissed me, he just wants to go farther and we end up in a wrestling match." explained Lulu.

"How much did your mother tell you about sex, Lulu?" asked Grammy.

"She just told me that I had better save myself for marriage or I might have a baby." answered Lulu.

"How do you feel about Jerry? asked Grammy.

"I don't know. He says that if I loved him, I'd go all the way, but I'm afraid to do that, so I guess I don't love him, but I'm also afraid I'm going to give in, 'cause I want to do it too." explained a blushing Lulu.

"No need to be embarrassed dear. Believe it or not, I can still remember that powerful urge when I was your age. So, do you want me to tell you what I see as your choices?" asked Grammy.

"Please do." Lulu quickly answered.

"Of course, you can choose to stop seeing Jerry at all," Lulu began shaking her head no, so Grammy continued, "Or you could see him less often and always in public places, preferably with others around."

"I could try, but he always manages to find a way to get me alone and it's really hard saying no to him. I don't know how long my will power will last." said Lulu.

"Then you'd best be prepared. Do you know about condoms?" asked Grammy.

"Kinda, but I don't know how they work." mumbled Lulu.

"Then it's time you learned. Go to the pharmacy and buy some Trojans and I'll show you how to use them." said Grammy.

"Oh Grammy, I couldn't. I'd be too embarrassed." Lulu objected.

"You'd be really embarrassed if you became pregnant, wouldn't you. Alright, then you have to hope that Jerry knows what he is doing and that he'll use them. Those are your choices as I see them." Grammy declared.

"Grammy, what do you think I should do?" asked Lulu.

"I think you should listen to your mother and the next time Jerry gives you that tired old 'if you love me' line, I'd tell him that if he loved you, he wouldn't ask you to do something you're afraid to do." advised Grammy.

Lulu reflected on Grammy's advice then hugged her, "Thank you, Grammy. I already knew what I needed to do, but I needed to hear it from a wise woman."

With only a few weeks until school was out, Lulu was confident that she could manage to keep Jerry at a distance.

Dinner hour was beginning to be more and more agitated as the war in Europe and in the Pacific escalated. Mr. Marshal would bring in large maps to illustrate where the action was happening, and the discussions were lively, with everyone given a say.

"We've already taken sides last January, when we passed the Lend-Lease bill to aid England and China to buy arms. Sooner or later, we'll be drawn into the conflict. I say that we should just declare war and get on with it." said Grammy one evening.

Another evening, Betty wondered, "I don't know why they haven't declared war on us. We've seized so many of their ships in our ports - 'under protective custody'. That seems to me to be a very belligerent thing to do."

Everyone had something to say on May 15 when a German U-boat sank a US merchantman and President Roosevelt declared an 'unlimited National Emergency'.

"That seems like an act of war to me. Why don't we just declare war and get on with it?" asked Lulu, echoing Grammy.

"I think it's a matter of diplomacy. Roosevelt is smart. I think he's waiting for them to declare war first, so they'll be the bad guys." was Mr. Marshal's answer.

"I think we've had enough talk of war. Who won the same letter contest this week, Grammy? asked Ellen, trying to change the subject.

Grammy answered, "I can't decide. Perhaps all of you could help me. I'll read them both to you and we'll vote."

Everyone agreed, so she got the folder where she kept the entries and shuffled through until she found the two she wanted to read. "I won't tell you who wrote them until after we vote." Grammy noted.

"This is entry one. 'Oliver overstuffed on oysters, oranges, oatmeal and olives before the opera. Observing the oboes through opera glasses during the overture and opus, he saw other options for his ocarina."

She paused for applause and laughter, then said, "This is entry two. 'Otis, in Otto's office, offered Otto the opportunity to own owls, but Otto already owned Ocelots, and Ostriches, Then Otis offered an option on an obsolete oil well and other outrageous opportunities in Omaha. Always optimistic. Otto opted to own."

The group voted for entry two, which Betty wrote.

After applause and congratulations, Grammy got the group's attention by tapping on her glass with her spoon. "This has been so much fun I'd like to propose that we all participate. The next letter being 'P', let's all write a 'P' story for the last week before summer. We won't judge them, but they will offer some levity to our last get together before we separate for a while.

The group was enthusiastic, and it was decided that everyone would participate.

When dinner was over, Betty and Lulu pushed Grammy back to her room.

"Please come in girls. I want to tell you how happy you two have made me. You know, Bruce's first wife couldn't have children, and I longed to have grandchildren. Now I have you and I couldn't be more pleased."

"Oh Grammy, we're the lucky ones to have you. I can't remember my grandmothers, so you're the only one I know." said Betty, putting her arms around Grammy.

"I remember one of mine, but you're much more fun and you don't dip that nasty snuff." Lulu said laughing and joining the hug.

After the girls left, Grammy dressed for bed and settled into her prayer and meditation mode, as she did every night before going to bed. She always expressed gratitude for the events of the day to a God of her understanding. Then she began to reminisce. After the love of her life was killed in an air crash during the war, she longed to have children, but she could not think of raising a child alone, so she entered into a loveless marriage with a man she felt would be a good father. As she reflected on the past, she gave herself credit for remaining loyal to the difficult man she had chosen to act as a father to her children. He had been an invalid for some time before his death. Grammy reflected that being a caregiver at her age had been very exhausting. After her husband's recent death, living with her son and his extended family had been the happiest in her life. She was finally surrounded by a loving family, including two caring teenagers, who served as the granddaughters she had been denied.

The last few weeks before school was out were very busy for Betty. The doctor, she would be working for in the summer, wanted her to get some training after school. Then she had to rush home to get her homework.

Lulu was busy too, trying to keep Jerry at arm's length. They were back to having the long conversations that Lulu enjoyed.

Mr. Marshal kept busy with meetings with other community leaders as they tried to anticipate changes they would need in case war was declared. He kept his ear to the news and made note of the latest news in Europe and the Pacific, making charts and maps to share with the others at dinner.

Ellen met with several organizations in the community and in her church. Many of the people she worked with on committees and such, were people who had shunned her when she was 'the young widow Brown'. She found it amusing that they couldn't understand why she would never join them in gossiping about others.

Grammy spent a good deal of time seeing doctors. She was finally able to walk again, but she was not as strong as she had been and wanted to become more self-sufficient.

No matter how busy they each became, they found time to work on their same-letter story. Any word beginning with 'P' was fair game. Some made long lists of 'P' words to inspire them. Others made up the stories and tried to tell it with all 'P' words. No matter the technique, they were enjoying the challenge.

The last week of May, a special dinner was planned to unveil the group's stories. When they finished an excellent dinner, there was the usual conversation about the latest news and what was happening with friends. Then Grammy took charge.

"I can't wait to hear what the rest of you came up with, so let's begin reading our stories. Since Lulu and Betty have experience, we'll let them start. Let's go from the youngest to the oldest. That makes Lulu first and me, last." pronounced Grammy.

Lulu got up, nervously shuffling papers. After clearing her throat, she began. "Pudgy Pamela, purchasing pasta, potatoes, pork, peaches, plums, and pastries to please her palette and plump her patootie. No participating in playing with people for Pam, she preferred passive pastimes, like putting pieces in pretty puzzles or playing a piece on the piano."

Lulu's story was met with enthusiastic applause and many complementary comments. Grammy said, "Lulu, you've set the bar pretty high for the rest of us. Let's hear what Betty has to offer."

Betty, buoyed by numerous contest wins, rose confidently and read, "Popular Pete, playing with proper pets like pussycats, but also pandas, pigs, ponies, and parrots, pleading with people to protect precious pets from pests and predators, playing polo in pools with porpoises. Proposing the pairing of people and pets for posterity."

When the applause died down, Grammy said, "youth has spoken. Now let's see what the older generation has to offer. Ellen, it's your turn."

Ellen was clearly nervous as she read, "Practical Pat, pleased with her purchase of pretty plants, planted them in pots on patio and porch, with purple petunias, pink pansies, passionate poinsettias, and proud peonies. Put practical plants, potatoes, pineapples, and parsnips, in plots in the pasture."

The group, knowing she had never done this before, was profuse in it's praise (this 'P' theme seems to be catching). Then Grammy announced that Bruce was next to read his entry.

Used to making speeches to large groups, Bruce used his best orator's voice to read his entry. "Poor Paul, passionate about poetry, not politics, but pulled to participate in both. Parents poo-pooed poetry and planned a political position for Paul, but Paul's preference was poetry, from Pope to Poe. To Paul, politics placed him in the public eye where the pavement is pitted with potholes of problems."

After the applause subsided, Grammy said, "I guess that leaves me. I must apologize to the youth in our midst for the risque content, but I think they are old enough to appreciate that kind of humor. Then she read. "Pretty Priscilla, Putting pride out to pasture by posing for pornographic pictures on posters, and a publication, 'Pussy Posse'. Her prudish parents pleaded passionately with Prissy, put a padlock on Priscilla's privileges and promised to punish if she partook, but Priscilla prevailed in pleasing people with her pulchritude."

Gasps and giggles had accompanied Grammy's reading and when she finished, applause was hearty and laughter prevailed. Bruce rose and took charge.

"Well, our endeavor seems to be a great success. Let's do it again this fall."

"I second that motion," said Grammy. "In fact, I think we should make a book of all the contest entries and the one's we did tonight." There was enthusiastic agreement with Grammy's suggestion.

It was the last week before summer break and dinner conversation centered around summer plans of the group, but especially around the fact that Lulu would be away in Austin. Betty reminded her that they had stayed close through letters before and could do it again. Grammy let Lulu know how much she would miss her, as did Bruce and Ellen.

Saturday was the last day before Lulu left and she had her usual date with Jerry. He had told her that he had a surprise, and he certainly did. He arrived in his parents' car. Lulu knew she had a struggle ahead, so she said,

"Great. Now we can drive over to Junction to the dance hall we've been wanting to go to."

"Sure," said Jerry, and off they went. When they got to a scenic overlook of the lake, Jerry pulled in. "I want you to see how pretty this is, and besides, we need to talk. You'll be gone all summer and I'm gonna miss you."

Lulu didn't object, because she would miss Jerry as well. When they got parked, Jerry moved closer. He said the steering wheel blocked his view. He put his arm around Lulu and she pushed him away, saying that she couldn't see with him so close.

"So, what did you want to talk about?" she asked.

"Lulu, you know I love you. I can't think of anything else. I want to kiss you all the time, but I want you to kiss me back -like you meant it." With that, he gave her the most passionate kiss and they were both aroused, but when he developed octopus arms, Roman hands and Russian fingers, she began to struggle. By then he had unzipped his fly and with penis in hand was trying to remove Lulu's panties.

"Please Lulu, help me. I'm in pain. I just want to rub it on your pussy - please."

"But you won't go in?" Lulu asked.

"No, no, anything just hurry." Jerry groaned

"Do you promise?" she asked.

"Yes, yes. Look, you can hold it and move it where you like," he bargained.

Lulu reluctantly lowered her panties and spread her legs, hoping he would be satisfied. There was not much room in the front seat, as it had a stick shift in the middle between the driver and the passenger. Lulu moved as far as she could away from the shift and Jerry balanced precariously over her, putting his penis in her hand. They were both aroused as she rubbed his penis over her clitoris. He was moaning loudly and she was cooing softly, when suddenly his body fell upon hers, pushing his penis into her vagina and trapping her hand on his penis, so he could not penetrate her completely. She howled in pain and pushed him away with all her might.

His head hit the rearview mirror above the center of the windshield. As his penis emerged, it was shooting semen all over Lulu and the car.

Lulu screamed, "You lied to me. Take me home you jerk. I never want to see you again." Jerry tried to make himself heard, but Lulu was hysterical.

"Take me home NOW. "

All the way home, Lulu sobbed and tried to rid her clothing of Jerry's residue, while Jerry apologized and made excuses, "I'm sorry, I slipped. I lost my balance. It was an accident."

Lulu remained unmoved. When they arrived home, she slammed the door as she left the car.

Bruce and Ellen were in the living room and heard the car door slam, so they went to the front door.

A disheveled Lulu entered and brushed past them saying, " I need to talk to Grammy."

A distraught Jerry followed Lulu in, but stopped to apologize to Ellen and Bruce. Ellen interrupted his apology to exclaim, "Jerry, you're bleeding. Did you have a wreck?"

"No, we had an argument." was Jerry's answer.

"Let's go to our apartment and I'll take care of your wound. You can tell us all about it." Ellen said.

Jerry knew he wasn't going to tell them anything, but he went with them.

Meanwhile, Lulu had burst into Grammy's living room, calling Grammy.

When she appeared, Lulu ran to her and put her arms around Grammy, who put her arms around Lulu , and tried to sooth her. Between sobs, Lulu blurted, "Oh, Grammy, Jerry lied to me. He told me he wouldn't go in me and he did and when I pushed him away, this slimy stuff squirted out of his penis all over me and the car."

Grammy looked into Lulu's eyes and asked, "Do you think some of his semen might have gone inside you?"

"I don't know, Grammy. It could have." was Lulu's reluctant answer.

"Then we need to try something. Some people think a vinegar douche will help get rid of any danger of pregnancy. It's worth a try." Grammy said as she moved toward the bathroom to prepare the douche.

"Lulu, would you go in the kitchen and get a bottle of white vinegar." she said over her shoulder. When she reached the bathroom, she took out her hot water bottle, which served many purposes. When filled with hot water, it could warm your feet or any other part of your body, and it had different attachments which would allow one to either give an enema or take a douche.

When Lulu returned with the vinegar, she watched Grammy's every move. As Grammy attached the hose to the water bottle, she pointed to a clamp. "All you have to do is release this clamp and gravity will do the rest," she said as she hung the bottle on a hook above the toilet and left Lulu to do her job.

When Lulu finished, she found Grammy and gave her a big hug, "Oh Grammy, thank you so much for being here for me. I could never be this open with my mother."

"You don't know how much it does for me to have such a beautiful young soul trusting me with her secrets. You're the granddaughter I wanted so badly." answered Grammy. "There's just one thing I ask of you, that you let me know immediately if you are late with your next period. Promise?"

"I promise, but let's hope that doesn't happen." Lulu said as she picked up her purse and moved to the door. " I've kept you up past your bedtime, so I need to go."

"Just a doggone minute young lady. You don't think I'm going to let you leave without giving me a big hug, do you?" Grammy chided.

"You'll get your hug when I tuck you into bed. Are you ready?" asked Lulu.

"As ready as I'll get. Let's go," answered Grammy, and off they went to the bedroom.As she left Grammy's rooms, she had to pass Betty's room and saw light under the door. Without thinking, Lulu found herself knocking on Betty's door. When Betty opened the door, Lulu hugged her, saying, "Oh, Betty, I've been such a fool. Forgive me."

A surprised Betty answered, "whoa, backup. What's the story here?"

"I'm just apologizing for all the time I've been spending with Jerry, when I could have been spending it with you. He's turned out to be a liar and I never want to see him again."

"What happened to cause all this?" a puzzled Betty asked.

"I'll spare you the details, but I'm over Jerry. I'll never trust another man after this." Lulu vowed.

Betty put her arm around a distraught Lulu and led her to the sofa, comforting her as they walked. "Oh, Lulu, just because Jerry has disappointed you doesn't mean that all men will do that. As for spending time with me, I don't have much time to spend with anyone, what with school and working, so you don't owe me an apology."

"But--but I thought you loved me and were jealous of Jerry," Lulu puzzled between sobs.

"I do love you and I was jealous of Jerry at first, but I guess I'm growing up, 'cause I finally realized that love and sex are separate things." explained

Betty. "I just want you to be happy. I'm so sorry Jerry's let you down."

Still sobbing, Lulu embraces Betty, "Oh, Betty, this is such a relief. I've always loved you in my heart, more than I love anyone else, but I just can't see myself loving you the way Rachel does. I want to be with you always, but not that way."

Betty embraces Lulu, savoring the moment, and whispers softly in her ear, "There, there, darling. Don't cry. I'll never leave you or ask you to do anything you don't want to do. We can work things out."

Lulu savors the safety of Betty's arms around her, then she stiffens and pushes away. "It's not fair!"

"What's not fair?"

"Just when things seem to be going good again, I have to go to Austin for the summer." was Lulu's answer.

"Honey, we can't do anything about that tonight, so let's just enjoy each other's company. I'm hoping you'll spend your last night here with me." soothed Betty, pulling Lulu closer.

"I'd love that," whispered Lulu.

Early Next Morning - June 1, 1941

Betty, fully dressed for work, touches Lulu's sleeping shoulder, "Lulu, honey, I have to go to work now. I won't be here when you have to leave."

Lulu is startled and sits up, saying, "Wha--Oh no. I'm not ready to say goodbye."

"I'm sorry, dear, but I can't be late, the doctor depends on me." answered Betty.

A disappointed Lulu answers, "Well, I guess we'll just have to write each other like we used to. I want to kiss you goodbye, but I think my breath smells bad, so give me a big hug, please.

A grateful Betty embraced Lulu, and murmured, "Thank you for letting me hold you last night. I haven't slept like that in a long time."

"And I want to thank you for restoring my trust - at least in women." answered Lulu.

Betty laughed, "I guess I'll have to address that last remark in my first letter."

After Betty left, Lulu went back to her room and started packing for her trip to Austin. She was making slow progress, as she had accumulated so many items she wouldn't need this summer, when there was a knock at the door. Glad to have a reason to stop packing, she rushed to the door and found Grammy holding some cardboard boxes. "I thought you might need these. You could store the things you won't need until you get back in school."

"Grammy, you must be a mind reader. These solve my problem. Come on in and let's have something to drink and talk," Lulu urged.

This is what Grammy wanted to hear as she would miss Lulu and was a bit concerned about her. "You know you're leaving a big hole in my days. I guess I'll have to use that time writing you letters."

"Oh, I'd love that," Lulu said, giving Grammy a hug.

"And Lulu, you won't forget about letting me know if you miss your period?"

"Oh, Grammy, I'm ok. "

Grammy changed the subject. "When are you leaving?"

"Pretty soon. Your son wants us to get an early start. It's so nice of him and his wife to drive me to Austin." Lulu answered as she started putting items she had set aside, in the boxes that Grammy brought.

"I think they want to meet your mother and hear some good music and Austin has plenty of that." said Grammy.

As Lulu continued to pack, they had a meeting of the Lulu and Grammy Mutual Admiration Society. Lulu was almost finished when there was a knock at the door.

Bruce entered, and, trying to be jovial, said, "Is my favorite adopted daughter ready to travel?"

"I guess I'm ready, but I'm going to miss you all, specially you, Grammy," Lulu answered as she gave Grammy a long hug, then she grabbed her bags, and off

she went, following Bruce and Ellen, without looking
back.

10

THAT AFTERNOON IN AUSTIN

Lulu was always a bit embarrassed by her mother's poor English and country ways, but the Marshals didn't seem to notice and were very cordial.

"We're going to miss this girl. She's been a wonderful addition to our family." said Ellen.

"Well, I can really use her here. A three-year-old takes more energy than I got." replied Lulu's mom. "Besides, I just took on a part-time job at the bakery and she'll have to take care of Tommy when Dorothy is at work too."

Ellen wanted to say that it didn't look like much of a vacation for Lulu, but she didn't. Instead she turned to Lulu and gave her a hug. "We will miss you, dear. If you want to come visit any time, we'll come get you and bring you back."

"That's so nice. I'll be tempted, but I'll write as often as I can. Sounds like I'm going to be kept pretty busy." Lulu said as she hugged them both.

The Marshals said their goodbyes to Lulu's mom and off they went.

A Week Later

Lulu woke up Friday and realized that she didn't have her usual cramps.

She hoped that didn't mean that her period would be late. She knew that might mean that she was pregnant. The thought of telling her mother sent her into a nose dive wishing to be near Grammy instead, for help and consolation, so she did something she would never do ordinarily. She made a long-distance call to Grammy. Such calls could be very expensive in those days. When a surprised Grammy answered, Lulu dissolved into tears, but managed to convey that she needed to be there with Grammy.

"Lulu, please try to calm. Perhaps we can take care of your concerns over the phone," Grammy urged.

"No, Grammy, My period is late and I need to be near you. Please try to persuade my mom to let me return to the Marshal's," Lulu managed to get out between sobs.

"Lulu, dear, you must try to calm down. I'll talk to your mother and try to convince her that you are needed here even more that she needs you there. It won't be easy, so be patient and do your part," Grammy said, trying to impress Lulu to stay calm.

June 10, 1941

Lulu is back in Kerrville, lying in her bed in her old room surrounded by the family. Betty is holding her hand. "How did you convince Lulu's mom that she should be here, Grammy?"

"I didn't have too. Lulu was hysterical, so I convinced her mother that I was doing her a favor. I also pointed out that neither she nor Dorothy needed to work since their husbands provided quite well for them and that neither of them had worked before Lulu had arrived, so either of them could afford to quit." Grammy laughed. "Any way, she's here now and we need to get her to a doctor to verify if she's pregnant. I'm overdue for a checkup, so we can go together."

So, the rest of the week was spent making a doctor visit, where tests were made on both Lulu and Grammy, and rearranging rooms so Betty and Lulu could have adjoining rooms, because Betty insisted that Lulu needed her attention.

When the family next met for dinner, Betty revealed her intentions. "I'm so grateful to all of you for rescuing my truelove. I'm going to take care of her and the baby. Together, we can be a family," Betty cooed as she rubbed Lulu's hand.

"Don't you think that's going a bit far?" asked Bruce.

"Son, times are changing. Not all men are as responsible as you. There are plenty of examples of households being run by two women. They just don't advertise it," Grammy answered for Betty.

Betty agreed, as she stroked Lulu's hair, and added, "And I know of at least two couples, all men, who are raising children together. They just quietly take care of children that would otherwise be institutionalized."

"That's hard to believe," said a skeptical Ellen.

Betty offered, "I'll be happy to introduce you to one of those couples.

Dave and Fred are good friends of mine. They were living separately, but as a couple, when Dave's sister and husband were killed in a car wreck, leaving two children to Dave, who was his sister's only living relative. The authorities were alright with that, but he put Dave on probation. He hired a female nanny and the probation ended. So, Fred took the nanny's place, and they have been a happy family ever since."

"I hope you all can understand my wife's and my reluctance to accept a definition of family that isn't headed by both a male and a female. This is the example set by our church and what is traditional practice in our society," Bruce offered. "We've just never known of any situations like you describe."

"Don't be too sure of that," Betty answered.

"Yes son, you know how we were questioning the arrangement Lillian Jackson has with that really masculine woman. After Lillian's husband died, that woman moved in and they seem to be raising Lillian's children together," Grammy chimed in, "They just don't advertise that they are a couple."

Betty has been becoming increasingly impatient with the conversation and finally bursts in, "I'm sorry you feel that way Mom and Dad, but I love Lulu and whatever she is facing ahead, I'll be by her side supporting her. I was hoping my family would back me up. If not, Lulu and I will go it alone."

"Betty dear, we all want to support Lulu in every way we can, but can't you see that your plan would rob her of finding a father for the child to come." Ellen reasoned with her daughter.

Lulu, who had been silent during the conversation, spoke, "Never!

I'll never marry a man. Don't trust 'em,"

"There, there, darling you mustn't get excited again. We're all just expressing opinions, we have to listen to others if we expect them to listen to our views," soothed Betty.

Betty turned to the others, "Perhaps we should continue this conversation later. I think Lulu needs to rest ."

As they were leaving, Ellen took Betty aside to say, "Honey, I hope you know that both your father and I will stand behind you and Lulu no matter what we might feel about your arrangement."

"I appreciate that, Mom. Family support is so important to us both."

Grammy piped up, "and I want everyone to know that I am supporting Betty and Lulu's version of a couple, not something made up to look good for the Church folks."

Betty, anticipating an argument, urged, "Please, could you continue this outside. Lulu really needs to rest."

Grammy apologized for her outburst and parted peacefully, Betty quickly went to Lulu's side and stroked her hair. Seeing that Lulu is agitated, Betty reassured her. "Don't worry darling, my family will pull together behind us.

We've been through the gossip mill before and it's made us stronger as a family."

The next night when the family was gathered for dinner, Bruce announced the results of the tests made at the doctors. "The tests showed that mother's blood pressure is dangerously high. The doctor prescribed pills to lower her blood pressure, and told her to rest."

Betty spoke up, "I'm getting tired of doctors in this country thinking pills are the only way to cure people's problems."

"What would you suggest, dear?" asked Ellen.

"I think Grammy could benefit from a better diet and exercise in addition to the medication. I've been doing a lot of reading about how other countries practice medicine. Our medical books hardly mention diet or exercise, but other country's medical books stress them both."

"I don't like to exercise and I like the way I eat," was Grammy's reaction.

"I know how you feel Grammy. Betty tells me that I need to eat better and exercise more. The tests the doctor took showed that I am pregnant for sure. Maybe we can exercise together," Lulu suggested.

"Sure, we can share our misery, and I'll talk to a dietician about how we should eat," Grammy answered.

"That's the spirit - teamwork," said Betty, hugging them both.

A Week Later

Betty sat down next to Lulu and put her arm around her. "Honey, we need to talk about making some changes. You know, you will be showing one of these days, and that will be a problem if we stay here."

Lulu broke in, "I've been thinking about that too. I won't be able to go to school without causing a scandal for your folks. I don't want to put them through that.

Betty went on, "It's not just that. I need to have a way to support you and the baby and I can't do that if I go off to college, like dad plans. I'm having second thoughts about being a doctor anyway."

"Oh, no, You can't give up your dream," Lulu pleaded.

"It wasn't my dream. It was dad's. Remember, I always planned to be a veterinarian, and this is my chance. I've been in touch with the vet I worked for when I lived with Julia and Vernon on their farm. He has a job for me and will help me get further training. You can go to school in Fredericksburg. I remember that there was a married girl who was pregnant in school when I was in school, and they won't know you."

"All that sounds good, but I can't leave Grammy. She needs me," protested Lulu.

"Lulu, Honey, Grammy hasn't needed you since the family hired that full-time nurse. It's you who feels a need for Grammy and you can write her or even phone. We need to do this so we can be self-supporting. Don't you see, I need to prove to everyone, including myself, that I'm capable of taking care of you and our baby?"

"Oh, darling, I have no doubts about you, but what about your dad? Won't he be very disappointed?

"You're right, Honey. I plan to have a long talk with him. I think I can apologize for deceiving him and convince him that this is the right thing to do - both for his family and for ours," was Betty's answer. "Maybe you should go with me to talk to dad."

When they got to her dad's door, Betty hesitated to knock. "Come on, Honey, Let's get this over with," urged Lulu.

Betty gathered her courage and finally tapped on the door, which was quickly thrown open. "What a nice surprise, a visit from the two beauties who always make me happy," Bruce said as he gave them both a big bear hug.

"Dad, what we have to tell you might not make you too happy, but if you let me tell you the logic behind our decision, I think you'll agree that our plan will benefit us all in the family. I just need to tell you the whole story before you interrupt. Agreed?"

"Of course, dear, but first, let's all get comfortable," said Bruce.

When they are all seated, Betty began, "I'm sure that you are aware that Lulu will be showing before very long. This will mean no school for her and a lot of gossip in the community. My solution to that is for Lulu and I to go elsewhere, and I have it all planned. First of all, Dad, I'm going to have to disappoint you. I need to drop out of going to pre-med school."

Lulu can see that Bruce is about to object, so she intrudes, "Betty doesn't really want to be a doctor, she dreams of being a veterinarian."

"Honey, this is not about my dreams, I need to earn a living for you and the baby somewhere besides here," Betty explained to Lulu and turned to Bruce. "Dad I have a job with the vet I was working for before you and mom married. Remember, when I lived with my sister Julia and her husband, Vernon, on his family farm near Fredericksburg?"

Bruce was becoming very agitated. He jumped to his feet and confronted Betty. "You deceived me! I distinctly remember you saying that you dreamed of being a doctor."

"You're right, Dad, I did say that. Please sit down and let me explain," urged Betty. Bruce remained standing. "When we first talked about your helping me with college and you suggested premed, I told you the truth - that I had wanted to be a doctor when I was growing up, but I was so eager to please you, that I omitted that my wants changed when I was introduced to veterinary medicine. It was an error of omission, not done to deceive you.

I knew it would make you and mom proud to have a doctor in the family, so I went along with your plan. Now, I'm the head of my little family and I have to do what's best for us. And dad, I think it will be the best thing for the rest of the family. I don't want mom to have to go through that gossip mill again, and I'm sure you don't either."

Lulu interrupted, "Honey, I think we should give your dad some time to digest this. Let's plan to talk again soon when we know more about our move. Is that alright with you, dad?" Mr. Marshal nodded sadly.

Betty turned to Lulu and said firmly, "Lulu I already know all there is to know. I start my job at the vets next Monday. "

Lulu gasped, "Oh no, I can't leave Grammy so soon. We have plans to help each other get healthy together."

"Maybe it's best for you to stay here until you start showing, I will be busy for a while," assured Betty.

Besides working for the veterinarian in Fredericksburg, Betty had made a bargain with her brother-in-law, Vernon. In return for letting her and Lulu live in a cabin on his farm, Betty would build a storage shed for all the items that had been stored in that cabin.

So, for the rest of June and July, Betty and Lulu lived apart, but visited each other as often as Betty could get away. Lulu and Grammy took long walks every day and found more active pastimes than they had previously done. Lulu no longer spent hours reading and Grammy stopped lying around so long listening to the radio. In addition, they consulted a dietician and changed to a more healthy diet.

As July neared it's end, it was time for Lulu to go live with Betty, who had finished getting the cabin ready. School would be starting soon and even though she would be showing, Lulu wanted to enroll in school in Fredericksburg.

The night before Lulu would leave, the family had a farewell dinner.

Betty had come to help Lulu move. The Marshals had come to terms with the situation even though they had doubts that it would be wise for two women to try to raise a child.

Fortunately, the subject didn't come up. Bruce was upset by the prospect of our country being drawn into war. "I can't believe Roosevelt would freeze Japanese assets and cut off access to our oil. They were already threatening us for cutting off shipments of scrap iron, steel and airplane fuel last year. Now that Japan has an alliance with Germany, they're going to pull us into war one way or the other."

Ellen put her hand on her husband's arm. "It's Lulu's last night here, so let's talk about more pleasant things. Grammy, have you told everyone your good news?"

"The doctor says my blood-pressure is down to normal. Those long walks with Lulu paid off," replied Grammy.

"Oh Grammy, that's wonderful," exclaimed Lulu. "Now you've got to promise me that you'll keep up the exercise and I will too."

"Good. And don't forget, we changed the way we were eating too. I miss all those sweets and bread, but to my surprise, I'm beginning to enjoy more vegetables." answered Grammy.

Everyone laughed when Lulu said, "I eat them, but I can't say I enjoy them. Maybe I can figure out a different way to cook them when I start cooking."

"Have you both decided that you would do the cooking?" asked Grammy.

"No, I decided. Betty will be working to put food on the table, so it makes sense that I will do the cooking and cleaning," answered Lulu.

"That's nice to hear. I've been trying to do it all until you got there and it's not that easy. It makes me appreciate when I lived here and had all those things done for me. Thank you, Dad and Mom, for allowing Lulu and me to share your hospitality for so long," said Betty.

"This is your home. You're both welcome here any time." answered Ellen.

"That's right," agreed Bruce. "Any time you need to come home, I'll come and get you."

"Thank you, dad. Now, we need to get to bed. I know it's early, but I need to go to work in the morning. So we need to say our goodbyes tonight, 'cause we need to leave before the crack of dawn tomorrow."

"Oh no," cried Grammy. "I'm not ready to say goodbye."

"I'm not either. I'm going to miss you so much Grammy," said Lulu as she hugged Grammy.

"Fredericksburg is not that far away, so we can visit often, and you can always write," assured Ellen.

"And your rooms will always be waiting when you can come." added Bruce.

"We'll come back as often as we can. We'll both miss you all I know." said Betty and Lulu agreed.

August 1941

While waiting for Lulu to join her, Betty had some time to adjust to having to do everything for herself, but the first month held a challenge for Lulu. She was never allowed in the kitchen when she was growing up so she never learned to cook. Fortunately, Betty's sister, Julia lived nearby and was willing to help her learn.

Betty had more experience around the house, as she and her sisters had done all the cooking and cleaning while their mother was at work, but she had a full- time job now and could only tell Lulu what she remembered.

Toward the end of August, Lulu was getting the hang of housework but she wanted to enroll in school in September and wasn't sure she could do both.

Betty encouraged her to go to school, "I'll help you around the house.

We won't starve. You need to get your education. But Lulu, I have to point out that you are beginning to show a little. We need to have a story to tell people. I told Julia that your husband died in a car wreck, so maybe we should stick to that."

"Oh Betty, I don't want to lie about it," protested Lulu.

"I don't see another way to avoid your being shunned by everyone, I don't think society is ready to accept our situation yet," replied Betty.

The last weekend in August, Betty and Lulu went back to visit the Marshals. Dinner was lively. Betty explained, "We thought we'd better come to see you before school starts. Lulu's been busy learning to cook and when school starts, we won't have time to do anything but survive burnt dinners."

Lulu objected, "That's not fair! I only burnt dinner once and that was because you had brought in that little orphan lamb for me to bottle-feed."

Grammy interrupted, "It's so good to see my little walking buddy. Lulu, I want you to know that I take the same walk we used to do every day and I feel great."

"I don't take walks anymore. I get plenty of exercise cooking and cleaning. Besides, with all the animals around I'd have to watch where I step. There are no sidewalks on the ranch," countered Lulu.

"Lulu, I've been meaning to tell you that your friend, Jerry, asks about you every Sunday at church. He wants to see you while you're here -says he owes you an apology," offered Ellen.

"Well, I don't want to see him. I'm not mad at him anymore 'cause I've thought about it and I have to admit that I let him get into a position where he could slip, so I have to share the blame for what happened," said Lulu.

"Do you think Jerry knows that Lulu's pregnant?" asked Betty.

"I don't think so," answered Ellen.

Betty turned to Lulu. "I wonder how he'll react when he finds out-especially if he hears our story that you were married and your husband was killed in a wreck."

"Maybe I should see him at church and tell him that I'm pregnant and see if I can get him to go along with our story," Lulu answered.

"Honey, if he sees you at church, he'll know, so you need to call him and see if you can meet somewhere before that," was Betty's reply.

Bruce has been listening to the conversation, "If this boy has any manly instincts, he won't be happy with your story. After all. He planted the seed and he'll want to get the credit. It's his child too."

Betty's jaw dropped in amazement, "Dad, I can't understand the way you men think. If they think they have equal rights about a child, let them carry it in their body for nine months, nurse it and care for it til it is grown. I'll grant you that they earn the living, but many women do that too."

Ellen, knowing her husband's need to always be right, interceded, "Betty, you shouldn't speak to your father like that."

"I'm sorry, dad, I wasn't directing that at you," said Betty.

Before Bruce could answer, his mother spoke up, "It's getting late, and we all have a full day tomorrow, so I say, that we save any more conversation for the next time we meet."

Betty couldn't wait until they got to their room. When they were halfway down the hall, she turned to Lulu and asked, "What did you mean that you let him get in a position to slip? You told me he put it in without your permission."

"Well, he did. I just left out that I let him rub his penis on me as long as I held on to it. In thinking back, I can see how he could have slipped. He was balanced over me and we got pretty excited." explained Lulu.

Betty stopped and turned to face Lulu. "You lied to me."

"No, I didn't. I just left something out, like you did when you didn't tell your dad about wanting to be a vet," replied Lulu.

A furious Betty turned and started to walk away, then turned back.

"Lulu, I need some time to myself. You stay here. I'm going back to the ranch tonight."

An astonished Lulu couldn't decide what to do. They had never had an angry exchange. They always talked their differences out calmly. Lulu stood there bewildered until she remembered that Grammy lived just down the hall. Soon, she was knocking at Grammy's door.

By the time Grammy opened the door, Lulu was crying uncontrollably,

"My goodness child, what's the matter?" she asked.

"Oh Grammy, I've lost my best friend," Lulu cried.

Grammy put her arms around Lulu and led her to the couch saying,

"Now you just sit here and try to calm down while I make us some hot cocoa. Then you can tell me all about it." Lulu nodded.

By the time Grammy brought the cocoa, Lulu was calm enough to tell her what had happened. Grammy reassured her saying, "Lulu dear, Betty is just jealous that you gave Jerry a privilege that she wants and she is angry, but she'll get over it. Give her some time."

True to her word, Betty went back to the ranch early the next morning, leaving Lulu at the Marshal's. The following morning, Lulu decided that she needed to tell Jerry about the baby before he found out another way, so she called him. He agreed to meet her after work at Pete's Pit, where they used to go. She went early so she could hide her condition until she was ready to tell him.

When Jerry arrived, he looked around for Lulu, but the only girl her age there had short hair and had on no makeup. She looked larger than he remembered Lulu. When she waved at him, he rushed over and gave Lulu a big hug. The male touch still excited her and she hugged him back. As he sat down, he said, "I almost didn't recognize you with your hair cut short. Your hair was so beautiful. What made you cut it?"

"Oh, Betty and all her friends have short hair and it's so much easier to keep. You've changed too. You're taller and seem more sure of yourself. I'd tell you that you're better looking, but I don't want you to get the big head."

Changing the subject, Jerry asked, "Does this meeting mean you're not still mad at me?"

"I've thought about it a lot and I realize that I agreed to let you be in a position where you could slip, and I believe you when you say that's what happened." said Lulu.

"Great, now we can forget the whole thing!" said Jerry as he moved in for another hug.

"Not so fast Jerry, I have something to tell you." said Lulu as she revealed her condition. "I'm pregnant."

Jerry backed off, unable to speak. He sat down as though he had been punched in the stomach and was finally able to say, "What are we going to do?"

"WE are not going to do anything. Betty and I have a commitment to raise the child together. She's mad at me now, but she'll get over it." explained Lulu.

"Don't I have some say in this? It's my baby too." sulked Jerry.

Suddenly, he brightened up. "We'll get married. I'll quit school, get a job, and my parents will help. They're always after me to get married and have them some grandchildren."

"I can't do that. Betty and I have it all planned. We are going to raise the baby together and tell everyone that my husband was killed in a car accident." explained Lulu.

"Lulu, the baby needs a real father. Let's get married" begged Jerry.

"Jerry, I need to go talk with Grammy. I didn't expect you to act like this and I'm confused." Lulu explained. "Let me think about it tonight and we can meet tomorrow at your lunch hour at the Pit."

"OK," said Jerry, "but don't be late, 'cause I only have an hour for lunch."

When Lulu got back, she went straight to Grammy's apartment and told her all that had gone on in her meeting with Jerry. "Grammy, I don't know what to do. I agree that my baby needs a real father, but I've made a commitment to Betty, but Betty's mad at me and she may not want me to be with her anymore. So, what should I do now?" pleaded Lulu.

Grammy's answer came quickly. "You need to find out where you stand with her. My son said he'd take you any time, so I'd go to the ranch today and see if Betty is over her anger. You have a lot to iron out."

Lulu didn't hesitate to act upon Grammy's suggestion. She was in luck.

Ellen had been wanting to do some shopping in Fredericksburg and Bruce was willing to take off work for the afternoon, so they were soon on their way. The conversation as they drove was lively. Lulu told them what Jerry had proposed and Bruce approved heartily, but Ellen was concerned that Betty would be so hurt if Lulu broke the comitment she had with her daughter.

When they neared the ranch, Lulu asked to be dropped off at the gate so she could surprise Betty. The plan was that Bruce would then drive to Fredericksburg with Ellen to shop and they would come back later to visit with Betty and Lulu.

As Lulu approached the cabin, she was pleased to see Betty's car, so she decided not to knock. As she burst through the door, she yelled, "Surprise!"

At first there was silence, then a bustling sound coming from the bedroom. Soon, Betty appeared tying the belt on her robe. "Oh, you were asleep. I'm sorry I woke you." said Lulu.

"I wasn't asleep. Why didn't you call first?" asked an irritated Betty.

"Honey, I wanted to surprise you." answered Lulu.

"Well, you certainly managed to do that." snapped Betty. Then she quickly changed her tone. "Look Lulu, I've tried to do things your way. I could teach you my way of making love and we could both be happy. Oh, what the heck," (calling) "come on out Rachel."

Lulu was so surprised, she couldn't move until Rachel came out of the bedroom in only a slip and said, 'Hi Lulu' in a tone that said, 'I won'. This infuriated Lulu and she turned around and walked outside. Betty followed her. A distant flash of lightning, followed by the sound of thunder, could be seen on the horizon.

Please Lulu. I don't love Rachel. I love you, but I've been so frustrated sexually, I called Rachel. It was just sex." pleaded Betty.

"I don't care what it was. You've broken our commitment (A brighter flash and louder thunder) Good. It saves me from being the one to do it first. Jerry has asked me to marry him and I'm going to say 'yes'."

"That's not fair!" cried Betty.

"Life's not fair, Betty. I think it's time we thought of the baby. I don't think I love Jerry, but It will need a real father. After all, It's Jerry's baby too, and we won't have to be lying to everyone about a dead husband."

A tearful Betty has been shaking her head in disbelief as a horn is heard at the gate. It's Ellen and Bruce. who have heard that stormy weather is on it's way, so they decided to visit first and shop later so Lulu could go with them. Lulu ran to the car, got in and urged Bruce to turn around, but Betty followed Lulu and grabbed the car door handle. Ellen turned to Lulu and asked, "What's going on here?"

"Ask your daughter," replied Lulu.

Ellen rolled down the car window and asked, "Betty, what's going on here?"

"Lulu says she's going to marry that boy. Please, come in the house and let's talk about it." pleaded Betty.

"I won't go in that house as long as Rachel is there." snarled Lulu.

Bruce interjected, "You two need some time to cool down, so why don't we take Lulu shopping with us. It will give you time to send this Rachel person away, Betty. Then we can come back and have a civil conversation in comfort."

Ellen could see by the way she was shaking her head 'no', that Lulu didn't like that idea, so she said, "We can talk about that on our way. (a nearby flash of lightening and a loud clap of thunder) That storm is getting near. I think we should skip shopping and head for home."

Lulu added, "And Betty has made her choice, so there's nothing here we need to talk about."

"Majority rules", said Bruce, "Kerrville, here we come."

As they drove, Lulu told them all that had happened and both Bruce and Ellen agreed that Lulu had made the right decision.

"Oh, no, you don't understand. I haven't decided to marry Jerry - just that I won't go back to Betty," corrected Lulu.

"But the baby will need a father," countered Bruce.

"And Jerry is his real father, and such a nice boy." added Ellen.

"I know, but I need to get to know him better. I want to marry for love and I'm not sure how I feel about Jerry right now."

"You need some time to get to know each other better. Why don't you come live with us. We could use some help with Bruce's mother. She's more feeble than she will admit. She adores you and you have a good influence on her. She says that being around young people keeps her feeling young."

Ellen said as they drove back to Kerrville.

"That would be perfect. Thank you so much. I wasn't looking forward to going back to Austin to baby sit my nephew." a joyful Lulu said.

When they got back, Lulu went straight to Grammy's room to tell her all that had happened with Betty at the ranch. They both celebrated the good news that she would be living in the same house and available for those long walks they both enjoyed so much. When Lulu told her about her decision to get to know Jerry better, Grammy lit up like a Christmas tree and said, "I like that boy, but you're smart to take it slow. Of course, you know that my family will always stand by you and help you take care of the baby if you decide that you won't marry him. So, what if people gossip."

This reminder of what would befall the family if she didn't get married made Jerry seem more important. She suddenly remembered that she had missed the date she had made with him for lunch, so Lulu excused herself, saying, "Grammy, I'm suddenly exhausted. I need some time to sort things out. Save some time tomorrow for a nice long walk." They hugged and said goodnight.

Lulu rushed to her room and called Jerry to apologize for standing him up. His mother answered and Lulu identified herself and asked to speak to Jerry. When he came to the phone, he snarled, "Why did you stand me up?"

"I'm sorry, Jerry, I had to go out of town suddenly." Lulu answered.

"You could have called. You know you've always taken me for granted and I'm tired of it." He continued, "I'm not sure I want to marry someone who has so little respect for me."

Lulu was at a loss for words. She'd never seen this side of Jerry. "I don't know what to say, Jerry. I respect you. Look, I'm really tired and confused. Can we talk about this tomorrow?"

There was a long pause. Then Jerry grumbled, " I'll call you," and hung up.

Lulu hung up and sank, exhausted, into bed. She was on the edge of sleep, when a disheveled Betty burst into the room. "Please Lulu, let me explain." Lulu couldn't muster the strength to resist, so Betty continued. "I missed you so much and I was so frustrated, so when Rachel called, I let her come by. She has a girlfriend now, so I thought it would be just a friendly visit, but things just got out of hand. It was just sex, Lulu. I don't love Rachel. I love you."

"We had a commitment," a feeble Lulu managed.

"I was getting to that. I want us to make a new commitment - to be true in love, but free to deal with our frustration."

Anger and disbelief fueled Lulu's response, "So you'd be alright with me having a roll in the hay with Jerry, as long as it was just for kicks?"

Before Betty could respond, Lulu added, "and I've been dealing with my frustration just fine. As long as I have money for batteries, I'm OK. Now, get out of my room or I'll scream."

Betty knew that Lulu meant it, so she fled from the room. Lulu quickly locked the door and collapsed on the bed. She was so exhausted, she soon fell into a state of fitful dreaming that she was lost and couldn't find her way home.

Betty stood, bewildered, in the hall. She hadn't seen this side of Lulu in a very long time-in fact, since they were kids playing cars. Lulu would threaten to tell Betty's mother on her if she didn't give Lulu her way.

Thinking of this made Betty yearn for the reassurance of her mother's arms, so she moved on down the hall and knocked on her door. When Ellen opened the door, Betty hugged her mother and burst into tears - something she hadn't done for some time - and felt her mother's warm, comforting arms fold around her.

Lulu awoke the early the next morning to her phone ringing. It was Jerry, calling as he said he would. As soon as a sleepy Lulu answered, he said, "Lulu, meet me at the Pit at noon. I only have an hour for lunch, so don't be late." Then he hung up.

This woke Lulu up and she was tempted to call him back and give him a piece of her mind, but she decided to talk to Grammy first.

When Grammy saw that it was Lulu, she was pleased. Lulu apologized for visiting so early, but Grammy said, "Nonsense. I was just ordering breakfast, so I'll ask for two. Now get comfortable and tell me all about what is obviously bothering you."

Jerry's hang up call was fresh in her mind, so Lulu told Grammy about his new aggressive behavior toward her.

Grammy thought a minute and said, "You know, it sounds to me like he is trying to behave more manly, like he thinks a father would. You need to nip that rude behavior in the bud if you think you might marry him. I'd leave him waiting at the Pit and when he wants to know why. I'd tell him that you want the old Jerry back."

"You know, Grammy. I think you're right. He's told me that his father acts like that. You've been a big help with Jerry, but I can't see any solution for how Betty has changed. I need your advice"

Lulu then launched into a full account of surprising Betty with Rachel, and Betty's plan for an open sexual agreement in their domestic arrangement.

When Lulu finished Grammy said, "I'm not surprised. You both have such differing needs and expectations that I doubt if you could ever agree.

It's a shame, because you both love the other in your own way, but you make much better friends than partners. You really need to make peace with Betty. You have been friends for so long. It would be a shame to grow apart now when you need that friendship. You just have to be very clear that you can't remain a couple under her conditions."

"Oh Grammy, I know you're right. I need to apologize to Betty for being so rude to her."

"That's a good idea," said Grammy. "Now, you're asking me for advice, so here goes. This is how I see things. You need time to sort things out, so I suggest that you stay here with us and go to school here. My family will take care of you and the baby, along with who you end up with."

Lulu threw her arms around Grammy and exclaimed, "Oh Grammy, That is so generous of you. But I don't want the gossips to have a field day, so I'm still going to tell everyone that my husband was killed in an accident."

"Maybe that won't be necessary if you can get the old Jerry to come back" was Grammy's sly answer.

Lulu took Grammy's advice to stand Jerry up, meanwhile she decided to call Betty and apologize for yelling at her. When Betty answered, Lulu said,

"Betty, I apologize for being so ugly to you. You're my dearest friend and you don't deserve to be treated that way."

"In this case, I think I did. We need to talk about this. Could I come over?"

"Sure. We have a lot to talk over," said Lulu.

Knowing that it would take Betty a while to get there from the ranch, Lulu decided to visit with Grammy.

As soon as they sat down, Grammy asked, "Have you heard from Jerry yet?"

"Nope, but I called and apologized to Betty and she's on her way here." was Lulu's answer.

Grammy was pleased. "Good. The two of you need to iron out your differences. You've been best friends too long to let a failed plan spoil it."

"I agree. Well, I'd better get back. Jerry might call." said Lulu as she headed for the door.

While waiting for his call, Lulu armed herself with a comeback when he would ask her why she didn't show up. She would say, "I don't do command performances," but that angry call didn't come. Instead, when Jerry called he sounded like the old Jerry. "Lulu, I don't blame you for not meeting me. I realize now how I must have sounded. See, I've been listening to these older guys at work. They're always saying that a guy has to show women who's boss. I tried, but I don't like me when I treat you that way. I still love you Lulu, so please don't be mad at me."

This was the old Jerry, and Lulu melted. She invited him to come over and talk about it. He thought she meant now, so he said, "I'll be right over." and hung up before she could object.

Lulu started to dial back to tell Jerry that Betty was on her way over, when there was a knock on the door. It was Betty.

"Come on in and make yourself comfortable. I have to call Jerry back to tell him not to come now." offered Lulu.

"Why don't I go visit with Grammy. I wanted to talk to her first anyway.

"You can call me when he leaves." offered Betty and off she went.

Lulu got dressed and prettied up as quickly as she could. She was still combing her hair when Jerry knocked.

When Lulu opened the door, Jerry gave her a big hug and said, "Oh Lulu, I prayed you wouldn't be mad at me and it worked."

"Jerry, sounds like you're still on a spiritual path. Have you started going to church?" asked Lulu.

"No, I just keep reading Grammy's poem and reading books along the same line. Oh Lulu, I've missed having you to talk to," whispered Jerry as he took Lulu's hand in his.

Jerry's touch gave Lulu that old thrill and she realized that he had not changed. He still loved her. "I've missed our talks too, Jerry. I hope we can start taking those long walks again."

Great, lct's start as soon as I get off work." Jerry looks at his watch. "Oh my gosh, I'm gonna be late to work. Is it a date?"

"It's a date," smiled Lulu as she closed the door. Lulu decided then and there to go back to writing in her spiritual journey journal.

Lulu couldn't wait to tell Grammy how the old Jerry was back, so she knocked on her door, but there was no answer. Lulu then knocked on the Marshal's door. When

Bruce opened it, Betty was there. Bruce told Lulu that Ellen had taken Grammy to the Doctor as she had a fainting spell.

Bruce was leaving to go to the hospital, so Lulu and Betty went back to Lulu's room. The first thing they did was to say a prayer that Grammy would be alright. They reflected on how dependent they were on Grammy's wisdom.

"You know. Grammy says that you and I make better friends than partners." said Lulu.

"I guess she's right, but I wish we could work something out where we could be a couple and raise this baby together." answered Betty.

"I haven't ruled that out, but I have to decide if that's in the baby's best interest. There's something to be said for having a real father, you know." said Lulu.

"When are you going to decide?" asked Betty.

"I don't know. I need to get to know Jerry better and find out how I feel about him. Are you going back to the ranch tonight?" asked Lulu.

"I was hoping you'd let me stay here with you tonight," answered Betty.

"Sure. Why not. You can sleep on the sofa." was Lulu's answer.

"On second thought, I think I'll head for the ranch" said Betty, and off she went.

When the Marshals returned, Ellen reported that the doctor said that Grammy was malnourished and dehydrated. Lulu decided that she would have meals with Grammy so she could encourage her to eat and drink more.

So, Lulu settled into a pattern of meals with Grammy and long walks after dinner with Jerry. Lulu told Grammy all about how Jerry was back to the loving boy he had been. "If you want to see for yourself, he would like to visit you." said Lulu.

"That would be nice. How about tonight after dinner?" Grammy answered.

That night, Jerry was on his best behavior, knowing how Lulu listened to Grammy's advice. "How are you feeling Mrs. Marshal?" Jerry asked.

"Full! Every time I turn around someone tries to get me to eat something, or drink something. I feel like a stuffed turkey." was Grammy's answer.

"Well, you certainly look better," Lulu laughed.

Grammy wasted no time with small talk. "I understand you want to marry Lulu and be the father to her baby."

"I am the baby's father. It'll be my baby too." stated Jerry. "I want to take care of it and Lulu too."

"Have you talked to your parents about getting married?" asked Grammy.

"My folks approve of us marrying and they will help us if we need it." assured Jerry.

Lulu changed the subject. "Grammy, Jerry wanted to talk to you about what you said in your poem. We talk about things like that all the time."

"It's so good that you are tending to your spiritual needs." said Grammy.

"Let's the three of us get together and have a discussion about what I said in the poem. I'm not feeling well, but let's make it soon."

Lulu sensed that Grammy wasn't up to their visit, so she said, "Jerry, I think we need to get going on our walk. I want to get to bed early tonight."

Jerry agreed and turned to Grammy, "It's nice to visit with you Mrs. Marshal. I hope you feel better."

"Thank you, Jerry. You two have a nice walk. Good night."

It was a breezy November night and they kept up a brisk pace with little conversation. When the walk was over, Jerry put his arms around Lulu and said, "Lulu, please let me really kiss you like I want to."

"I'm afraid you'll get carried away, Jerry."

"No I won't. Just kiss me back, please," and with that, he pulled her body to his and kissed her long and passionately. Gradually she responded. When he finally came up for air, Jerry whispered. "When we're married, we won't have to stop."

Lulu pushed away saying, "Jerry, you take it for granted that I'll marry you. I'm still not sure. Two people should be in love when they marry."

"I love you Lulu. I have for a long time." Jerry vowed.

"But I'm still not completely sure how I feel." answered Lulu. "Give me time."

Early the next morning, Lulu knocked on Grammy's door. "Come in," called Grammy.

As soon as Lulu was in the door, Grammy said, "I was just ordering breakfast. What will you have?"

"Whatever you're having," answered Lulu. "I wanted to see if you are feeling better and ask your advice."

"I'm feeling much better. So sit down and tell me what's on your mind."

"You know Jerry is after me to marry him and I'm just not sure that I love him." Said Lulu after she got comfortable.

"What makes you think that love is a requirement for marriage? Most marriages are based on need and you certainly need a father for your baby.

Perhaps you should consider the child's welfare first." was Grammy's no nonsense advice.

"Did you marry for need or love, Grammy?" Lulu wondered.

"Neither. I married for want. I was almost thirty and I had this strong urge to have children, so I was looking for good daddy material, not a love interest. When I met my future husband, I knew he was going to be the father to my children, so I chased him til he caught me. He was so handsome, I knew he'd make beautiful babies, and so smart and reliable that he would be a good provider. Though I didn't totally love him when I married him, I grew to love him dearly." was Grammy's frank answer.

"So you think I should marry Jerry." said Lulu.

"I didn't say that. I merely told you what I think about marrying for love." responded Grammy. "You have to decide that for yourself."

That night, Lulu couldn't sleep. She thought about her feelings for Betty.

They were deeper than what she felt for Jerry, but the sexual pull she felt for Jerry made up for that. She loved their long walks after dinner. They held hands and had interesting conversations on topics like the possibility of war and spirituality, not just idle banter. At the end of the evening, Jerry would kiss her goodnight and they both would be aroused, but didn't follow through. It was becoming harder and harder to resist temptation - for both of them. Then she reflected on what Grammy had said about not having to marry for love, and decided to seriously consider Jerry's offer of marriage, but first, she wanted to have the family get to know him, so she invited him to dinner that night.

When they arrived, Mr. Marshal was trying to convince his wife that war was imminent. "Ellen, I know what I'm talking about. FDR just placed the Coast Guard under the direction of the US Navy, and that is only done in a time of war."

"I'm sure you're right dear, Look, Lulu has brought a friend to dinner," soothed Ellen.

Lulu and Jerry are deep in conversation with Grammy across the room.

"How are you feeling Mrs. Marshal? The last time we spoke you weren't feeling well."

"I'm doing quite well, Jerry, and I wish you would call me Grammy so Ellen won't think you're talking to her."

A confused Jerry answered, "I don't think I understand that."

"She means that Ellen is also Mrs. Marshal, silly. She's teasing you, which means that she likes you." explained Lulu.

"Thank you - Grammy. My parents taught me to respect my elders. They wouldn't approve of my calling you by your first name, but I'll call you Grammy because you asked me to." Jerry explained.

The Marshals have joined them and Grammy says, "Jerry here is the real Mrs. Marshal and her husband.

Before Jerry could reply, Ellen said, "What is that about Grammy?"

"Oh, just a little joke I played on Jerry to get him to call me Grammy," said Grammy with a grin.

"Well, it's very nice to meet a young man with such good manners, said Ellen shaking his hand.

Mr. Marshal shook Jerry's hand as well and said, "Don't let my mother's sense of humor scare you off. Lulu needs a father for that coming attraction." The women all shake their heads in disbelief that he had said that.

"Thank you sir. I need all the support I can get in convincing Lulu to marry me." said Jerry.

Grammy to the rescue, "Dinner must be getting cold. Let's move into the dining room."

Both Lulu and Jerry were expecting to be grilled about a possible marriage, but dinner conversation was dominated by Mr. Marshal's dire warnings of impending war. It was late November, 1941 and he was predicting war by Christmas.

When Grammy could get a word in, she asked, "Son, don't you think Germany is already spread so thin that they won't declare war on us? We've been making all those Lend/Lease agreements with Russia and other countries that Germany is fighting. It keeps them busy on so many fronts. I doubt if they have the resources to open another one. Besides, after ignoring that U-boat torpedoing our destroyer last month, I don't think Roosevelt will be provoked into declaring war on Germany"

"I'm not talking about Germany. Don't you remember? I was telling you last summer about the embargos FDR has put on products that Japan needs to fight China. Now Japan and Germany have formed an alliance. I'm more worried about Japan than I am Germany, but the two countries could keep us busy on two fronts and win a war and they know it."

"Darling, can't we talk about something else. I'm so weary of all his speculation. I think our president is too smart to be dragged into declaring war." urged Ellen.

"I agree with you, Mrs. Marshal. We've been at peace all my life, and President Roosevelt is really smart. He's the only president I can remember." Lulu declared.

Grammy turned to Jerry and asked, "What do you think about all this young man?"

"Well, I talk to my dad a lot about it. He served in the last war and he thinks a lot like Mr. Marshal. My mom is worried that I would be drafted to fight if we went to war." answered Jerry, cleverly side-stepping what he thought.

"Your folks sound like sensible people. I'd like to meet them. Bring them to dinner soon," said Paul.

"Thank you sir. I will." added a pleased Jerry.

Across the room, Grammy was saying to Lulu, "When you've said goodnight to Jerry, come by my room and we can talk."

"Could we make that in the morning, Grammy? I really look forward to my goodnight talks with Jerry, and we have a lot to talk about tonight. I want to brag on the way he's been with the family and reward him with a sweet, goodnight kiss."

"It sounds like you're warming up to Jerry."

"Yes I am," replied Lulu. "I've even had some sweet dreams about him - and some others I won't mention." Seeing Jerry nearby out of the corner of her eye, she adds, "Oh, I hope he didn't hear that."

"Hear what?" Jerry asked as he moved closer.

Grammy answered, "Lulu was just saying something nice about you."

Jerry put his arm around Lulu and teased, "I think I need to get you outside so I can properly thank you for your kind words. But first, I want to thank the Marshals for having me."

As Jerry went across the room to speak to the Marshals, Grammy urged Lulu to make her decision soon.

As soon as Jerry and Lulu got outside, Jerry took her in his arms and asked tenderly, "Well, did I pass inspection?

"With flying colors," cooed Lulu. In fact, I'm ready to give you an answer."

Jerry kissed her passionately, then said something surprising. "Wait, I want our engagement to be something we'll always remember, so let's make a date for tomorrow night at the steakhouse. I'll make reservations for one of those private tables with the soft lights and you can give me your answer then. I have to see my folks first, so I think we need to say goodnight now."

After a lingering kiss, Jerry left Lulu standing outside the dining room.

She decided to go back in and talk to Grammy.

When she found Grammy, Lulu said, "Grammy, I can talk tonight after all."

"Fine, but I think you ought to know that Betty is here and Rachel is with her." answered Grammy.

A surprised Lulu said, "That's fine. I was hoping they would get back together."

"I think I understand. Let's go to my room and you can tell me what you mean." a puzzled Grammy said.

When they were seated and Grammy poured some tea, Lulu began,

"I guess I was unrealistic, but I didn't want to make a decision about Jerry as long as there was even a small bubble of hope that Betty and I could work things out."

"You'd better make that decision soon. By my calculations, you're seven months along. Wearing looser clothes won't change that." advised Grammy.

Before Lulu could answer, there was a knock on the door. Lulu went to open it for Grammy and there were Betty and Rachel. Expecting fireworks, Betty turned to leave, but Lulu said, "Come on in. I'm glad you've made your choice. It frees me to make mine."

"You mean you're not mad anymore? "asked Rachel.

"Not a bit. I'll always love Betty in my way, but I can't give her the kind of love she wants. You can and I'm happy for you both," was Lulu's answer.

Grammy called, "Come on in girls and have some tea."

When they were settled, with tea in hand, Betty spoke, "Rachel quit her job and has moved in with me at the ranch. Rachel is a fabulous cook and housekeeper. She'd make the perfect wife - in every way, if you get what I mean."

With a wry smile, Grammy said, "I'm afraid I do." Grammy looked around at the three girls and said, "The way you all talk about it in innuendo makes me think that your generation thinks it invented sex. I'm going to tell you a story about how lack of sex - affected me when I was your age.

11

GRAMMY'S STORY

The war was raging and I was deeply in love with a young soldier named Rube. He was in officer training school at the University of Texas. I worked after school at a bookstore, but most every night, we went out dancing. I was a 'good' girl and 'good' girls in those days, saved themselves for marriage, which meant, no sex without a marriage license. I'll let this poem I wrote, tell the rest of this story.

Dancing
"When I hear that SERENADE IN BLUE,
I'm somewhere in another world,
Alone, with you,
Sharing all the joys we used to know,
Many moons ago."
I can't be here when that music plays
time warped to then - close
moving to his command
total sensuality - effortless sync
sometimes amorous - often playful
seldom was oneness lost -
invisible bands connecting
every part of our bodies
woven together by
unseen chords of melody
exploring, creating, teasing
burning with unrealized
longing for each other.
Had he lived to consummate that desire.
Had lives gone as planned,
Could such harmony

have ever lasted until
GOODNIGHT LADIES?

Her quavering voice caused her to pause for a sip of tea and to find a tissue for her tears. A teary Lulu joined her and said, "could I have a tissue too?"

"Of course, dear. I didn't tell my story to make you sad. I only wanted to show you that it's only the things you fail to do that haunt you, like my insistence on saving myself for marriage. I'll always regret that I didn't share myself completely with the great love of my life, before his death."

Betty rushed over and put her arms around Grammy. "Oh Grammy. I know just how you feel. That's the way I felt about never getting to make love to Lulu."

Grammy untangled herself from Betty's grasp and quickly set the record straight. "I assure you that I didn't have your situation in mind when I told my story. I was thinking that you all will later regret it if you weren't able to give someone in your life - unconditional love."

Betty and Rachel embraced and gazed at each other, seeming to say that they already love each other unconditionally.

Lulu grew thoughtful and said, "I told Jerry tonight that my answer will be 'yes' and I'll try really try hard to love him unconditionally."

"Then it was worth the pain of retelling my story. Now, we all have a lot to think about, so let's say goodnight," said a wistful Grammy.

Lulu couldn't sleep that night. She was concerned about what she could wear for her date with Jerry the next night. All her clothes were too tight and she had kept Grammy's sewing machine busy for the last three months letting things out, but everything she had, had reached its stretch limit.

The next morning at breakfast, she told Grammy her concerns. Grammy turned to Ellen, who was sitting next to her and said, "Ellen, Lulu needs to go into town to get something that fits her. I think she needs to get a maternity dress."

"She doesn't need to go to town for that. I have a closet full that I've saved. They should fit her and I don't think they ever go out of style," answered Ellen.

So, with the help of Ellen and Grammy, Lulu spent the rest of the day getting ready for her date with Jerry that night. She found just the right shoes to go with the maternity dress that Ellen gave her and Grammy sent her to the beauty shop to have her hair styled and makeup applied.

When Jerry arrived, he was obviously pleased with the way Lulu looked and the feeling was mutual. Jerry was dressed in his Sunday best, with a new haircut and a box under his arm, which he extended to Lulu, saying something he had rehearsed many times, "beauty deserves beauty."

Lulu had never been given a corsage before and didn't know what to do with it, so Jerry took charge. "I hope you like camellias," he said as he pinned the corsage on her coat.

"Oh Jerry, it's so beautiful. I want to show Grammy. She's in the dining room getting ready for dinner with her family. I hope you don't mind," enthused Lulu.

"Your wish is my command," said Jerry as he followed her into the dining room.

The group was not yet seated, so they gathered round Lulu and Jerry, complementing them on how well they looked together.

Ellen insisted that Lulu should wear the corsage on her dress instead of her coat and Lulu reluctantly revealed that she was wearing a maternity dress.

When Jerry saw this, he said to the group, "I had planned to do this at the steakhouse, but I think I need to get on with it." With that, he knelt before Lulu and said with a flourish, "Lulu darling, will you marry me?"

The group laughed, thinking that Jerry was joking about the maternity dress, but Lulu knew better and answered, "Yes, Jerry dear, I will."

There was an awkward moment for the group. They didn't know how to react, but Jerry did. He stood up and embraced Lulu. Then they kissed and the group burst into applause, which lasted until Paul raised his water glass and announced, "I'd like to propose a toast." He waited until everybody was able to get their water glasses. Then he grinned and said, "May the road ahead be smooth, and may the three of you travel it with love and in good health."

Lulu buried her head in Jerry's shoulder, and when Ellen saw this, she comforted Lulu by saying, "Don't mind my husband's offbeat sense of humor. We are all thrilled that you are getting married."

When Lulu raised her head, she revealed that she had been laughing, "I like his sense of humor."

"So do I, but we need to go. We have a reservation at the Steakhouse and I have another surprise for Lulu," added Jerry.

"Well, I don't want to delay you, but I'm so happy for you, I have to have a big hug from both of you before you go," urged Grammy.

All the way to the steakhouse, Lulu tried to get Jerry to tell her what her surprise was, but he just grinned and said, "It won't be a surprise if I tell you. Have a little patience."

When they were seated, Lulu turned to Jerry in anticipation and said, "Well?

Jerry answered, "A well's a hole in the ground. Now what are you ordering for your dinner?"

Lulu pouted, "I dunno."

"Then I'll order for you." said Jerry ignoring her attitude. They waited in silence until the food was put before them on covered dishes. Jerry removed his cover to reveal a sizzling steak and said, "Aren't you going to look to see what I ordered you?"

"I'm not hungry," Lulu mumbled.

"Then I'll send it back," said Jerry, "but at least look at it."

Lulu grudgingly lifted the cover and let out a squeal. In the center of the plate was a beautiful, old-fashioned diamond ring. "It was my grandmother's engagement ring. My mom wanted you to have it when you said yes," Jerry explained.

"It's so beautiful. Now, we're officially engaged," cooed Lulu.

"I hope it'll be a short engagement. My folks said if we do it before Christmas, they will foot the bill" Jerry added.

"That's wonderful. The sooner, the better." was Lulu's quick come-back.

"OK. How about next Sunday, the seventh?" asked Jerry.

"December 7, Perfect. We'll be married before Christmas!" exclaimed Lulu.

"Let's, go tell my folks. I'm sure they're still up," urged Jerry.

Jerry's parents were overjoyed at the news and reassured the couple that they would bear any expenses, but they said that they would be unable to help them with a place to have the wedding. It seems that their church had some narrow views on who could be married there and Lulu, in her obvious condition would not qualify.

Lulu said, "That's fine. I don't want to be married in a church anyway."

When she got home, Lulu saw a light under Grammy's door and decided to share her news. Grammy was pleased to see her. When Lulu told her about not wanting to be married in a church, Grammy suggested that the dining room there would be big enough and they decided, if Jerry agreed, to ask the family at dinner tomorrow if they would approve having the wedding there.

When the family gathered for dinner the next evening, Bruce asked,

"How many guests do you plan to ask?"

Lulu answered, "Not very many, just Betty and Rachel and a couple of school friends."

Jerry followed, "I'd have my parents and brother and his wife and one or two school friends."

Bruce responded, "Well, that's certainly doable. I say we have the wedding right here in the dining room. Hold up your hand if you agree." All hands went up and Lulu and Jerry beamed as they gave each other a hug.

Grammy suggested that the wedding service be held in the morning on Sunday the 7th so those who wanted to attend church later, could, and it was agreed.

With only a few days to prepare, everyone was busy. Ellen worked on decorating and planning the reception. Bruce planned the music and had the piano tuned.

Grammy, was in charge of finding a minister. Those who had congregations were reluctant to try to officiate at a wedding in the morning and preach a sermon a short time later. Fortunately, Grammy knew a retired minister, who she knew to be very broad-minded and he was available.

Jerry and Lulu, were in charge of invitations, which they hand delivered because of the short time until the wedding day. In addition to that, they were busy planning on what to wear in the wedding.

On the wedding morning, everyone was up early getting ready for the wedding at nine o'clock. Usual leisurely Sunday routines were abandoned - no reading the newspaper, or drinking coffee while listening to the news on the radio. The guests had gathered and at promptly nine AM, the music started, the bride entered, escorted by Bruce, to the side of an eagerly awaiting Jerry. The music stopped and the marriage ceremony began.

The text was traditional, familiar to all and was rendered by the aging minister in mellifluous tones. He had obviously performed this ceremony many times, over his long life. When he asked Jerry if he took Lulu to be his bride, Jerry's answer was overly emphatic, causing the audience to titter.

When it was time to exchange rings, Jerry had trouble getting the ring on Lulu's finger, causing another round of tittering.

No one noticed that an agitated member of the kitchen staff had entered the room and delivered a whispered message to Bruce.

The minister said, "I now pronounce you man and wife. You may kiss the bride."

At this point, the music was supposed to begin, when Bruce stepped up to the bandstand to make an announcement, but the band director objected. "Wait until she throws the flowers man."

Bruce objected. By then, the kiss, which was supposed to be interrupted by music, had gone on for longer than was comfortable to the couple, the Minister, or the audience, so the band director ignored Bruce and signaled the music to begin. Bruce shouted over the noise. "The Japanese are attacking us!" Only the band director was close enough to hear him and he stopped the music. So, Bruce continued, "Japanese planes are bombing our naval base at Pearl Harbor as we stand here. "They've interrupted all programming on the radio to cover the attack, so, let's get us a loud Radio in here and find out."

He headed for the kitchen to get the radio, followed by Mr. Jackson and his other son. Jerry stayed behind with his new bride.

Ellen and Grammy busied themselves with preparations for the reception.

Lulu looked at her bouquet and started to cry, so Jerry put his arms around her. Soon, Betty came over to comfort her, saying, "Don't cry honey. At least you are married. All you missed was tossing the flowers.

Here, throw them to me. I know, I'll never be allowed to marry Rachel, but I can dream."

This stopped Lulu's tears and, though she really didn't believe it, she said, "Don't give up hope. You never know what time will bring."

While Betty and Lulu were talking, several of Jerry's school friends had come over to congratulate him and to tell him that they felt that they needed to skip the reception so they could be with their families. Others left as well, so, when the men got the radio in place, it was just the family, Jerry's family, and Betty and Rachel who gathered around. Bruce turned up the volume and everyone hung upon every word. From time to time, someone would mutter things like, "Those dirty Japs" and "Only filthy cowards would pull a sneak attack." The announcers talked about the fact that the Japanese chose Sunday morning while many of the personnel would be off duty and maybe in church.

New news came in slowly, so when the commentators began repeating themselves, Grammy moved to turn off the radio, but her son objected.

Grammy countered with, "We've let this cowardly attack take our attention from why we gathered here. Let's try to focus on the important event that occurred here tonight- The marriage of two wonderful young people. Now Lulu didn't have a chance to toss her bouquet, so come on ladies let's get in line. Ellen, Jerry's mom, Grammy, Rachel and Betty were the only women left at the reception, but they gathered around and Lulu targeted Rachel, but she missed and, Jerry's mom caught it. She quickly tossed it to Betty, who handed it to Rachel, saying. "Let's hope you get to toss one some day at our wedding."

All the men including Jerry, watched the toss but quickly migrated to the other end of the hall, where the radio, now sitting on the bar, was still telling of bombing and strafing by the Japanese planes in Pearl Harbor. They kept the sound down - in deference to the women, who were still focusing on Lulu and the wedding.

Grammy was asking, "What will you name your baby, Lulu?"

"If it's a girl, we think we'll name her Elizabeth Ellen," was her quick reply.

Both Betty and Ellen gave her big hugs as they thanked her profusely.

Ellen was teary eyed, so Betty added a bit of levity. "You can call her 'Bettel' for short.

Grammy interjected, "If you do, some smarty will call her 'Beetle'."

When the laughter died down, Jerry's Mom asked, "But what if the baby is a boy?"

"Jerry wants to name him 'Jeremy Bruce' after his dad and Mr. Marshal," Lulu answered.

"Bruce will be so pleased. I have to go tell him now." Ellen enthused.

"I don't think Jerry has told Jeremy, so I'll go with you." said Mrs. Jackson.

Just then, a loud noise of groans and 'oh no's' could be heard coming from the men gathered around the radio.

"My curiosity is making it difficult for me to concentrate. Why don't we all join the men and find out the latest horror?" Lulu asked of the remaining group, and they all agreed.

Lulu rushed to join Jerry, who was pouring himself a drink at the bar.

After a warm embrace and kiss, Lulu said, "I didn't know you drank."

"I don't, but now that I'm an old married man, I thought it was time to see what I've been missing. Have one with me?"

"Don't mind if I do," giggled Lulu.

Ellen and Grammy moved to a large table near the radio.

Then she joined Bruce, who was at the bar having a drink. "Did Jerry tell you what they will name their baby if it's a boy?" asked Ellen. When Bruce answered 'no', Ellen told him, and he was so elated that he forgot how anxious he was about the news coming through on the radio and joined Jerry and Lulu to thank them.

When Mrs. Jackson told her husband about how the couple planned to name the baby after him if it is a boy, Jeremy said, "Jerry just told me and I'm headed for the bar to toast the choice with him."

"Jeremy, I never thought you would encourage our son to drink!" said his wife.

"Sarah, our son is a married man, capable of making his own decisions," countered Mr. Jackson.

Lulu listened to the accolades Bruce and Jeremy had in their toasts to her and Jerry for planning to name their baby after them, and said, "thank you both for all your kind words. I hope you'll excuse us. I need to sit down."

A concerned Jerry took Lulu's arm and led her to the table where Grammy was. She had been joined by Betty and Rachel. As Jerry helped Lulu sit, he asked, "Are you alright, Honey?"

"I'm fine. It's just that I'm a lot more concerned about the kind of world my baby will grow up in than what we'll name it."

"You should be concerned. The President will surely declare war now that we've been attacked," groaned Betty.

Grammy added, "The last war went on for years. All the young men were drafted and went to war. Women went to work in factories to take thier place. Just about everything was rationed. Your child will not grow up in the same kind of world as you two."

Lulu put her head on Jerry's chest, and he held her close. Between sobs, she managed to say, "Oh Jerry, I don't want you to be drafted and I don't want to work in a factory. I so wanted our baby to grow up in peaceful times, the way we did."

A wise Grammy tried to soothe Lulu with, "There, there dear. Don't cry.

We'll find a way to tell it all about your childhood."

Grammy found a way to tell Lulu's child about growing up in peaceful times. She wrote this book. You see, Grammy as well as Lulu are the same author-narrator, Patricia Sawyers Fiske.

THE END

ACKNOWLEDGEMENTS

FAMILY

The encouragement I have received from my daughter, Daryl, my son, Burch and my granddaughter, Maria, has been of tremendous help to me.

THE ALLEYWRITERS

When I started, I thought I was writing a memoir about Lulu (myself) and my friend, Betty, growing up in peaceful times; but when Betty was eight, and I was six, I moved away from Kerrville and lost touch with her.

The Alleywriters, my writing group, informed me that I would be writing a novel, not a memoir, because I would have to make up the rest of Betty and her family's lives if I wanted to continue with the story as I envisioned it.

The Alleywriters, had been invaluable to me in writing my first book, a memoir called, **Secrets I Couldn't Tell My Children**, so I trusted them to guide me in writing this book. Thank you Alleywriters.

SIDNEY BRAMMER

I have considered Sidney to be my mentor since the seventies, when I was still acting, she cast me in plays and films she had written. I began writing when she cast me in a play and told me that I had to write my part.

She was very helpful in the early stages of this book.

GEOFFREY HALL

I appreciate the help Geoffrey gave me when the book was in it's early development.

TERESA ORTA (TERRIE)

Terrie has been of invaluable help in getting this book together. Her many talents are much appreciated.

AUTHOR'S NOTES

In the two years since I started this book, the young people of my granddaughter, Maria's generation, have emerged as a national force to be reckoned with. They are marching in huge numbers to protest this government's inaction on several fronts. They don't seem to be letting up.

Perhaps growing up in times of belligerence has made them more aware of this country's failure to act on matters affecting them.

When I was young, our country and our people were the good guys in the eyes of most of the world. Now, it seems, that our people are widely hated because of unpopular policies of our government.

I think the actions of our young people are being noted by the rest of the world, helping show everyone that our present government does not reflect the thinking or the character of most citizens of America.